Second Event Chronicles

Marian Nichols
7-22-2007

Second Event Chronicles

By
Marian Nichols

E-BookTime, LLC
Montgomery, Alabama

Second Event Chronicles

Copyright © 2007 by Marian Nichols

All rights reserved. No part of this book may be reproduced or transmitted in any form or by any means, electronic or mechanical, including photocopying, recording, or by any information storage and retrieval system, without permission in writing from the copyright owner.

This is a work of fiction. Names, characters, places and incidents either are the product of the author's imagination or are used fictitiously, and any resemblance to any actual persons, living or dead, events, or locales is entirely coincidental.

Library of Congress Control Number: 2007932313

ISBN: 978-1-59824-533-2

First Edition
Published July 2007
E-BookTime, LLC
6598 Pumpkin Road
Montgomery, AL 36108
www.e-booktime.com

Proof Reader Review
of
Second Event Chronicles

Finished! Strong stuff, Marion.

Proof reading gives a very disjointed impression of the story, so, after two or three checking sessions, I read it straight through again. It shows a deep knowledge of the Bible and great imagination in the vivid unfolding of the story. The tension certainly builds up, to a surprising ending! It's very well researched too, and, I hope, now ready for publication. It must have been a lot of hard work and I wish you lots of success!
—— Anonymous

PS, - When you think about it, you and Dan Brown have something in common!
—— Anonymous

I dedicate this book to my sisters, for their help and support in the writing of this story.

I also wish to thank a certain couple, whose assistance made publication possible.

I dedicate it to both of my sons and my husband who believed in me.

Contents

Chapter One 11
Chapter Two 20
Chapter Three 30
Chapter Four 38
Chapter Five 47
Chapter Six 55
Chapter Seven 63
Chapter Eight 70
Chapter Nine 78
Chapter Ten 87
Chapter Eleven 94
Chapter Twelve 99
Chapter Thirteen 105
Chapter Fourteen 110
Chapter Fifteen 116
Chapter Sixteen 122
Chapter Seventeen 128
Chapter Eighteen 134
Chapter Nineteen 140
Chapter Twenty 146
Chapter Twenty-One 152

The Beginning of ... 'The Millennial Chronicles' 159

Chapter One

And ye shall hear of wars and rumors of wars: see that ye be not troubled: for all [these things] must come to pass, but the end is not yet.
   [Matthew 24:6]

The news had been alarming for quite some time now, even several years perhaps; it seemed as if the world had gone mad, at least to me. The events of 9/11 shocked the free world to its very core. I can remember very well that I was working in Carrie at the time, setting up a drug store with my company's new product line. I went into shock myself when I realized that there were people in this world that hated us that much.

Before these attacks on the US mainland, I hadn't paid too much attention to world events; I listened to what was reported but never gave them another thought... until 9/11!

Jet planes had been hi-jacked and then three of them were flown into the World Trade Center's towers and the Pentagon, bringing about these buildings' damage and destruction, and many deaths. One plane crashed into an empty field in Pennsylvania when the passengers rebelled, and the terrorist ditched the plane killing all aboard. This one was headed for the White

House. Perhaps God protected it for a reason. There were over three thousand people killed in these attacks! It wasn't until I arrived home that night, that I saw the horrifying scenes, that everyone was talking about who came into the store that day.

President Bush declared war on terrorism and on Osama bin Laden of Al Qaeda in particular. He started new programs, Homeland Security for one and the Patriot Act, another, to increase this country's security.

Afghanistan was invaded almost immediately, looking for bin Laden, and the Taliban government was overthrown when they did not hand over bin Laden. So the War on Terror began and things were changing in what was now becoming known as *the new normal*.

President Bush invaded Iraq in March of 2003, just two years after the events of 9/11, mainly on the premise of looking for weapons of mass destruction. The citizens and congress were in full support of this war at first and it seemed that we quickly came into victory. But that was far from the truth, and, although President Bush declared an end of hostilities only a few months later, we were still in Iraq and still fighting.

There had been kidnappings of foreigners and quite a few of these hostages had had their heads chopped off in front of a camcorder and the pictures were then posted on the internet for everyone to see.

I was seeing a part of man that more than a little frightened me, I was dismayed at the lack of love and compassion man was showing his fellow man, and all in the name of religion. A Jihad was declared on the USA and Israel, by Islam extremists, calling the United States the *Great Satan.* Sometimes I almost agreed, when I looked at how this country's morals had deteriorated to those of Sodom and Gomorrah of the Old Testament. *[Genesis; chapter 19]*

There had been continuous upheaval in the Middle-East ever since the election of Hamas to the Palestinian government, with Iran openly acquiring the means to produce nuclear weapons. This had the free world more than a little concerned.

Threats between the democratic nations and the Iranian government were flying, with sanctions being threatened by the United Nations and Iran promising *pain and harm* to those that enforced them, namely the United States. Although the United Nations was made up of one hundred and ninety one counties, or states, as they were called by the UN, the USA could not invoke sanctions of its own accord.

The war in Iraq seemed to be going well at times but then more insurgents' attacks would bring retaliations and it seemed to be a never-ending tic for tack, with more and more deaths for both the Coalition and the Iraqi people. The citizens were beginning to demonstrate openly against the USA and the Coalition, insisting that they leave Iraq now, although to do so would only lead to a government much like the one just ousted.

The trial of Saddam Hussein began. He had been captured less than a year later in Tikrit, his hometown. He was hiding in an underground hole, which was not much bigger than a prison cell; he had not managed to leave his country before or after the war started.

Although weapons of mass destruction were not found in Iraq, for which the Bush's administration took much heat, both from congress and the news media, testimony from Hussein's trial revealed that the ousted leader had intentionally sent out false communications, that he did indeed have weapons of mass destruction. He was hoping that the USA intelligence services, the FBI and the CIA, would intercept these lies and believe them, which of course is what did happen.

However, this did not do as Hussein had hoped, which was to deter the West from invading, for that is exactly what *did* happen. Of course, now that this had come out, only a few news sources and no politicians even so much as spoke of it, much less apologized.

In June of 2006 the most wanted Al Qaeda terrorist in Iraq, Al-Zarqawi, was finally located and two five hundred pounds bombs were dropped on his safe house. He was not killed instantly; he lived long enough to see the Coalition forces and know who it was that killed him. He attempted to get up from the stretcher he had been placed on but was too injured and collapsed and died.

For nation shall rise against nation, and kingdom against kingdom: and there shall be famines, and pestilences, and earthquakes, in divers places.
[Matthew 24:7]

Earthquake activities had been increasing and many countries were experiencing them, that never had before.

An earthquake beneath the Indian Ocean, December 26, 2004, produced a tsunami that destroyed thousands of miles of coast line along the small counties of India and most of the coastal cities, town and villages of other small countries. Many of them were wiped out completely, killing every living soul. It was reported that two hundred thousand lives were lost, making it the largest disaster in recorded history.

Second Event Chronicles

Even the planet itself suffered a blow and was thrown off of its axis by several degrees, with repercussions that remain to be seen.

The changes were subtle; our summers were melting into one another, bypassing winter. With this constant warmth in parts of the world that were not used to it, things were changing in the weather patterns and violent storms had begun wrecking the coastlines of the United States. Very large tropical systems at times were lined up across the Atlantic, taking aim on the southern coast and not giving any relief between the punches.

Louisiana had a category four storm which made almost a direct hit on New Orleans, in September of 2005. Katrina as she was named, devastated the below sea-level city, breaching the levees and flooding 90% of the city. Although ordered to evacuate, the poorest citizens couldn't and those that survived were trapped in their homes or on top of them for days.

There were also patients who were incapacitated, left in hospitals to fend for themselves and many drowned in their beds.

FEMA response was slow, bringing more criticism onto the Bush's Administration, and repercussions. Michael Brown was forced to resign and many horror stories came out of the hurricane's aftermath. Accusation of racism was screamed from all the news' networks because those mostly affected were the poor blacks of the New Orleans' suburbs.

Two major storms struck the Gulf of Mexico coast that year, one right after the other. Rita was the other hurricane, but that was not to discount the four storms that struck Florida the year before.

Millions of people had been displaced and for the first time in a very long time the United States was feeling very vulnerable, not only fighting a Third World

War (*at least I saw it as such, for we definitely were fighting a worldwide threat*) but now Mother Nature herself.

Because of the storms in the Gulf of Mexico, gas prices had almost tripled, which of course drove up prices for other necessities and commodities. It was a vicious circle with no end in sight.

April 2005 saw the death of Pope John Paul the 2nd and the election of Pope Benedict the 16th. This was not unexpected, for the Pope, John Paul, had not been in good health for quite some time. There was a sense that this new Pope would have a great impact on the politics of the world.

Since the early eighties, the world had been fighting AIDS, a virus transmitted by sexual contact, shared needles by addicts, and blood transfusions. This pestilence that began in Africa had rapidly spread around the globe.

It was first noticed in the United Stated by homosexuals using so-called *bathhouses* in California and quickly spread to the straight community.

The moral values in this country have gone down the drain. The *sexual revolution* began in the nineteen sixties and there has been no decline in its progress since.

More and more teens, girls as young as twelve are having sex and becoming pregnant at an alarming rate, making it more acceptable to be an unwed mother than ever before, often denying their children the benefit of a father living in the home.

Abortion is used as a form of birth control with the murder of the unborn, the slaughter of our country's most defenseless citizens, occurring thousands of times a day.

The infants of these very young unwed, mothers are often found dead, but sometimes still alive in trashcans. They throw away their babies like so much trash, without a second thought, as if they're just an inconvenience.

Couples do not bother to marry anymore; they live together without the blessing of God and choose to bring their children into this world and have the label, *bastard,* forever assigned to them.

Promiscuous sex, homosexuality, even bestiality, racism and bigotry are openly flaunted. Pedophiles seek out our very young children, use them and often murder them then toss their poor battered bodies in ditches along our major highways. They haunt our streets, our schools and now the internet, seeking young victims to satisfy their animal needs. More and more pornography, even child porn, grows like a cancer, overwhelming our law enforcement.

Crime is on the increase, murders, rape, drug use and theft has the average American hiding behind locked doors. We become prisoners in our own homes while the criminals roam free to carry out their most heinous of crimes.

The so-called *white-collar crime* in the last few years has come to the forefront. This type of behind the scene theft has largely gone unnoticed and unpunished with billions of dollars embezzled, leaving large corporations in the red and many of their employees with no jobs and a loss of their retirement plans.

Then there is *organized crime.* It has its hand in any type of underhanded scheme from drug importation, use, and sale to white slavery, where young girls are kidnapped and sold into brothels as sex slaves.

Percentages and statistics matter little, it all adds up to anguish and despair for the human race.

As of now, there is no hope for man, no release from his suffering. But out there, there are small groups of people fighting back. Keeping the faith and doing whatever they can to ease the pain of loss, despair and destitution, but these few are being overwhelmed and many that are religious-based are being mocked.

It is becoming harder for the Word of God to be taught as it becomes a mockery, for even religion [*Christianity or otherwise*] is tainted with preachers conning their congregations out of billions of dollars, more than the 10% asked for by the Word of God to help sustain the *true* Church.

Televised religion has become big business, where the common, honest, God-fearing man is lost, and left to fend for himself and his family alone.

For a nation that was founded on Christian values, a lot of the Christian symbols that are in place in many of our courthouses are being removed by court orders, such as the Ten Commandants from the steps of a courthouse in Alabama and even from the government itself.

In the fifties, in our schools, there was a prayer and a Bible reading that started each day, now, this has been stopped. Our forefathers, the founding fathers would turn over in their graves if they could see what this nation is becoming.

The words *politician* and *crook* seemed to go hand in hand with most of our leaders and we the people voted them there, having been deceived.

When we do vote for a person who stands on good Christian values, he is often criticized and scoffed at by those, who in their ignorance, cannot see, or will not see the good that they are trying to create.

This nation needs to return to the values that it was built upon and until it does, our God withdraws his hand of protection that we once enjoyed.

I might sound sanctimonious, but I do not stand in judgment of any man or woman, salvation is the responsibility of each individual. It is theirs alone and although they can be, and are informed, each one must choose for themselves, for no one can make this choice for them. I am only stating facts as I have seen them, even among my own family.

Now, there's a new threat on the horizon, the avian flu or bird flu, this virus is jumping species and should it mutate, it may gain the ability to be passed directly from human to human. The World Health Organization is preparing for a *pandemic*, but there are doubts that there will be enough vaccine and this strain is deadly.

We are nearing another hurricane season; I do pray we can be truly prepared for it.

Chapter Two

I began my life as the third child of Virginia and Woodruff Potter, July 14, 1947. I have four sisters, Anne, Clara, Larraine, and Ruth and three brothers, Colin, Drow, and Carter. Drow and Carter are the youngest with the five girls born between Drow and Colin who is the oldest. We sisters have always been very close and after the death of our parents, my home seems to be the meeting place for our family's get-togethers.

In August of 1948, I was seriously burned and nearly died. I spent a great deal of my early years in hospitals. I had a hard time in school, other children loved to tease me or make fun of me due to my having scars and the loss of the pinky finger on my left hand.

Due to long hospital stays as a child, I failed the second and the fourth grades, so I was fourteen in the eighth grade. I never did finish school or get a GED although if there is a subject I wish to know more about, or learn to do, I am generally capable of teaching myself.

I met Thomas in December of 1962 at the age of fifteen. We dated for seventeen months and married in May of 1964 when I was sixteen, just two months shy of my seventeenth birthday, and Thomas was twenty-four.

Second Event Chronicles

My first child was born only nine and a half months later, March 2, 1965, Thomas Jr. Art was born December 10, 1971 and Lance was born November 21, 1981.

I am mostly a passive sort of woman; I'm 59 this year, 2006. I have three sons; or rather, I had three sons, one deceased at the age of 20 in 1985. I lost him before I lost my parents. My father died two months later, and my mother died two years after that.

In my forty plus year marriage I lost two babies in miscarriages, the first one was in 1969 and the second one was in 1985, just four days before Thomas Jr. was killed. I consider myself as having lost three children instead of one.

Two of my sisters, Anne and Ruth both have lost a grandchild, and one sister Larraine, never gave birth but did adopt a son. So, Colin had three children, Anne had six children, Clara had four children, Larraine none but adopted one, Ruth had three children, Drow had two children and Carter none. My family is rather large and still growing.

My husband, Thomas, retired about three years ago, 2003, and I quit my job a year before that.

We had our first grandchild in the year 1996, when I was 49 years old. She was born of my son Art, her mother Sonja already had two children, one of which, the elder, was taken from her by Social Services and lived with the father's parents. Art and Sonja were not married, Sonja already had a husband who was doing time for drug trafficking. They stayed together as a couple for about two and a half years. They split due to Sonja having found another boyfriend, another drug dealer out of Florida.

Sonja left her children with a sister and headed for Florida. While she was gone, her sister reported her to

Social Services as having abandoned her children. The kids ended up in foster care. Art was unable to get custody of Lexis and asked that his father and I take her, which we did.

We decided to adopt her and in the two and a half years that it took, we learned that Art was not her biological father. Of course, we loved her and proceeded with the adoption, which was final in September of 2005. I now had my little girl, for whom I had longed each time I was pregnant. But I never did think I would have a little girl this way and not in my middle years, after my family was grown. We never know how our prayers will be answered. I see it as being meant to happen this way.

Lexis is very bright even though she has ADHD, Attention Deficit Hyperactivity Disorder. She is on two medications and is a very advanced fourth grader, making mostly A's on her report card.

Over the last few years my health has begun to deteriorate, I am over-weight and being a woman, I will not say how much, I don't mind telling my age but not my weight. I am diabetic, have high blood pressure and our old friend, arthritics. Two years ago, my right knee finally gave way and the left one is only a little better. I walk with a slight limp and use a cane at times.

My right shoulder aches almost constantly from a car accident I was in over twenty years ago. The normal aches and pains of growing older, limiting our ability to get around as well as we used to. None of us thinks we will ever age until one day, looking in a mirror or seeing yourself on video, you no longer recognize that person as being you. If you live long enough, you will experience the loss of loved ones, age creeping in and facing death. Suddenly you know you are mortal, you will grow old, that is if you are lucky, and you will die.

Is that all we have; birth, a hard life, and then death? This is where religion plays such an important part in people's lives, for it promises us that if we live a righteous life we will emerge from death with eternal life. Since Christianity is my religion of choice, I am more familiar with what the Holy Scriptures, the Bible, promises. I was raised as a Free Will Baptist and I was saved and baptized at the age of twelve.

I am very aware that other parts of the Earth observe and participate in other religions and I am not certain but I do imagine that all have a tale of a beginning, of an ending, and of an afterlife of sorts. I will deal with what I know and what I was raised to believe.

I attended church fairly regularly as a child and early teens, and was even married in the church I was attending at the time. I think I have a good knowledge of what the Bible tells us although there are only a few scriptures I know by heart and where they are located in the Bible. I know more than some but less than others. I have even studied outside of my denomination, from Jehovah's Witnesses to the International Church of God. I've even studied a little of the Catholic faith.

Which, you might think leaves me entirely confused on religion, no wonder so many people are agnostics or atheists. But I think that I am clear minded enough on the matter and that I can see through the frills and mysticism that surround religion.

We begin with Creation. The Creation of the Earth and the Heavens in Genesis, is more of a rebuilding of the Earth, after devastating damage was done to it, by the battle that was fought in the Universe, not just the invisible Realm known as Heaven. This battle occurred when Lucifer decided he should be as God and convinced a third of the angels to join him in rebellion for he coveted the very Throne of God.

Isa 14:13 For thou hast said in thine heart, I will ascend into heaven, I will exalt my throne above the stars (angels) of God:

John 3:16 For God so loved the world, that he gave his only begotten Son, that whosoever believeth in him should not perish, but have everlasting life.

As Jehovah has no beginning and no end, He is where all Universal matter and energy begins. God's first creation was his only begotten Son; created first and placed above all others. The word *begotten* in this sense means a direct creation by God; everything else was created through the Son, known as the **Word**.

John 1:1 In the beginning was the Word, and the Word was with God, and the Word was God.

John 1:2 The same was in the beginning with God.

John 1:3 All things were made by him; and without him was not any thing made that was made.

Rev 12:7 And there was war in heaven: Michael and his angels fought against the dragon; and the dragon fought and his angels.

The War in Heaven was won by the two thirds of the Heavenly Host that remain faithful and loyal to Jehovah and the Son. But it left the universe in turmoil and in devastation. Satan and his demons were cast out of Heaven and forbidden access to God's throne for eternity. He sought refuge on many of the planets in the universe and the Earth was one of them.

As Satan was once an Archangel, one of three, and was created as an immortal, he and his demons cannot be destroyed; they can only be restrained. There are only two remaining Archangels, Michael, and Gabriel. They now guard the way to God's throne, preventing Lucifer's return.

As our scientists have shown, the Universe is billions of years old; its Creator was before and will be after, the Universe.

Thus a rebuilding of the Universe was begun; there was much evidence of the battle everywhere, even appearing in our very own solar system. The warring factions used planets and stars as their weapons, as these were giants as compared to meager man, who would, billions of years later come on the scene. They had supernatural powers; they wreaked havoc in the Universe. Order had to be made from chaos, and this did not happen in seven, 24 hour days.

So through the Son, the Earth was rebuilt, and as time is meaningless to a Deity, a re-creation day was about seven thousand years long and, as we find stated in the Bible, a thousand years is like a day to God.

2Peter 3:8 But, beloved, be not ignorant of this one thing, that one day [is] with the Lord as a thousand years, and a thousand years as one day.

So the Earth was re-created, all plant and animal life had been placed upon this Earth, on the sixth day

Man and then Woman were brought into existence and God the Son, the Creator, rested on the seventh day, which is the Sabbath or Saturday. Sunday is the first day of the week and not the day the Son chose for a day of rest.

The creation week can be read in Genesis, chapter one through three. I will not post it here due to length. The Son said, "Let's create Man in our image." So, we know how God and the Son look, for we are made in their likeness.

The first Man was called *Adam*, the first Woman was *Eve*, and they were placed in a beautiful garden, The Garden of Eden and told that they could eat from all the trees there except one. In this garden were two very important trees, one was the **Tree of Life** and the other was the **Tree of Knowledge**. They were forbidden to eat from the *Tree of Knowledge*. They were told that should they eat from the *Tree of Knowledge* that in that same day they would die. The couple were completely naked but without shame.

God the Son blessed the couple and told them to be fruitful and to multiply, thus giving man and his wife the beautiful act of sex. *Sex was not the original sin.* Sex would also be very pleasurable for Man and Woman. In this fashion, the coming together of the couple would result in pregnancy and the sharing of genes of the couple making one, a child of their flesh. They would multiply and fill the Earth.

That is until Lucifer, also known as Satan the Devil, grew jealous. He knew God's plan for the human race. That plan was for humans to grow and become many and eventually to reach a status that would place them above the angels. They would have eternal life as long as the *Tree of Life* was available for them to eat its fruit.

The Devil is a liar, he is the inventor of the lie, and he lied to Eve. He took on the guise of a serpent and told her that God did not want them to eat from the *Tree of Knowledge* for God knew that in that day, they would not die but their eyes would be opened, they would know what God knew and become like God.

I do not think it is good to know what God knows. Our human minds cannot handle that much information.

Eve was weak and listened to Satan; she took the fruit from the *Tree of Knowledge* and ate it. She offered it to Adam and he ate the fruit and in the very second that they did, their eyes were opened and they knew. They knew they were naked and became ashamed and hid when God the Son walked in the garden that evening and called to them.

As an all-knowing Deity, God the Son already knew that they had sinned, the sin of disobedience. The original sin was disobeying God. He rebuked them and then God the Son cursed them, he told Adam that only by the sweat of his brow would he be nourished from the ground. Then God the Son cursed the ground and it was quickly taken over by weeds and brambles. Then God the Son cursed Eve, the Woman, and told her that her desire would be unto her husband and that he would greatly increase the pains of her labor and in agony would she bring forth children.

Next God the Son cursed the serpent, "On your belly will you go, into the dust of the Earth."

To Satan he said, **"And I will put enmity between thee and the woman, and between thy seed and her seed; he shall bruise thy head, and thou shall bruise his heel." Gen 3:15**

This is the first prophecy in the Bible and in it, the plan for Man's salvation began.

God drove Adam and Eve from the Garden of Eden, away from the *Tree of Life* and he placed two cherubs with flaming swords at the garden's entrance to bar Adam and Eve from ever returning.

Adam was a perfect human and when sin entered his life he lost his perfection and decay and death set in, and in that day, Adam died, just as God said. As a day is as a thousand years with God, Adam lived a long and hard life. Imperfection now tainted the genes of man; all of Adam's and Eve's descendants inherited this sin. They would all die. Lost to them was immortality. Lost was the closeness with their God and there was no way to regain it... or was there?

God the Son, would be born as a human; be conceived by the Holy Spirit into the womb of a human woman, a virgin. God would become flesh, He would dwell among Man, and He would be human. He would hunger, He would thirst, He would hurt, He would cry, He would love and He would suffer. Oh yes, He would suffer greatly and He would do it willingly to save His creation from eternal damnation and eternal death. He would not allow Satan to win.

The wages of sin is death, death without consciousness, dead is dead, and there is no thought in the grave. When a man dies, the spirit in him returns to God the Father, the One that gave it; it does not linger in limbo or wander the Earth as a ghost. Death is a deep sleep without dreams and no realization of the passing of Time.

What was lost in the Garden? A perfect life was lost. Satan now held Man as hostage and he demanded a ransom. A ransom he did not think could be paid. There was only one Being that could pay that ransom and that was God the Son. He threw off His Heavenly Glory and took on the lowly flesh of a human.

A perfect life was lost; a perfect life would have to be paid to redeem Man. The day Jesus Christ died on Calvary is the day that that debt was paid in full.

But that was not the end of it, no, Man had been redeemed but he must prove that he was worthy of that redemption, immortality does have a price. Now it would be hard for Man to prove his worth, especially since Satan as the god of this world taunted, teased, and tempted Man with every step he took.

With the passage of time, Satan kept the pollution of Man's DNA so that the worst of sexual pleasures grew and became vile and disgusting until the Earth itself was polluted with the filth of the soul.

The Word of God over the centuries has remained true although Christians have been persecuted, slandered, and slain in the name of their God.

Chapter Three

Neither shall thy name any more be called Abram, but thy name shall be Abraham; for a father of many nations have I made thee. Gen 17:5

As it had been laid out in the Bible, there came to be twelve Tribes of Israel. Abraham was father to Isaac, God found much favor in Abraham. When Abraham was willing to sacrifice his only son by Sarah his beloved wife, God knew He had found the source of the Seed.

Abraham did have another son whose mother was the handmaid to Sarah his wife. When Sarah found herself barren, she offered up her servant to Abraham so that he would have sex with her and produce an offspring. They had a son, Ishmael.

And Hagar bare Abram a son: and Abram [Abraham] called his son's name, which Hagar bare, Ishmael. Gen 16:15

However, God took pity on Abraham as he was righteous and told him that his wife Sarah, although she was well past her childbearing years, would conceive and bear a son who would be called Isaac and that from Isaac a great nation would arise.

Second Event Chronicles

After Isaac's birth, Sarah became jealous of Ishmael and forced his mother to leave with him, out into the desert where it was assumed they would perish.

And Abraham rose up early in the morning, and took bread, and a bottle of water, and gave [it] unto Hagar, putting [it] on her shoulder, and the child, and sent her away: and she departed, and wandered in the wilderness of Beersheba. Gen 21:14

But the servant with her young son prayed and God heard her and delivered her and Ishmael to safety where she was told that a great nation would come from her son. This was the founding of Islam, and many nations were a direct descendant of this child.

Gen 21:17 And God heard the voice of the lad; and the angel of God called to Hagar out of heaven, and said unto her, What aileth thee, Hagar? fear not; for God hath heard the voice of the lad where he [is]

But the promise of the Seed and the Blessing went to Isaac, who also had two sons, twins, Esau and Jacob, Esau was the firstborn and rightfully should have had the blessing and the promise of the Seed passed to him. But Esau sold his birthright to his brother Jacob for a bowl of pottage, a meat stew. With the help of Rebecca their mother, when Isaac was on his death bed and nearly blind, Rebecca fooled Isaac into placing his right hand on the head of Jacob and blessing him, passing the Blessing and the Promise of the Seed to the second born.

Jacob's name was changed to Israel, and Israel had twelve sons. But his wife, Rachel was also barren so the first ten sons were born of servants. Then God blessed Rachel and she bore Jacob, (Israel), two more sons, Joseph and Benjamin.

The older sons were very jealous of Joseph and they laid a trap for him and later sold him into slavery to a passing caravan of traders who were heading for Egypt. In Egypt, Joseph was sold again to a wealthy household.

Jacob was told that a lion had killed Joseph and dragged him into the bushes and devoured him. To prove this, the brothers slaughtered a lamb and smeared Joseph's coat of many colors with the blood, completely fooling their father, who went into deep sorrow and thereafter refused to allow Benjamin out of his sight for fear of losing him also.

In Egypt, Joseph was raised to a great position in the government when he interpreted two dreams for the Pharaoh; he told the Pharaoh that there would be seven years of plenty followed by seven years of famine.

You can read the whole account in Genesis chapters 31 through 50.

Joseph married the daughter of Potipherah, the priest and she bore him two sons. Their names were Ephraim and Manasseh, and as was the case with Esau and Jacob, the firstborn son of Jacob, aka, Israel, passed the Blessing and the Promise of the Seed onto the twin sons of Joseph. He blessed both boys and when it came time to lay his hands on their brow; he crossed his hands and laid his right hand on the brow of the youngest, Ephraim.

"And Joseph said unto his father, "Not so, my father: for this [is] the firstborn; put thy right hand upon his head." Gen 48:18

And his father refused, and said, I know [it], my son, I know [it]: he also shall become a people, and he also shall be great: but truly his younger brother shall be greater than he, and his seed shall become a multitude of nations. Gen 48:19

Later on you will see just who these two nations are and why it is important to know. Remember Ephraim was the younger son but received the main blessing.

I will not dwell much now on history in the Bible, we are where we learned of the **Twelve Tribes of Israel**, I will list them.

Asher, Benjamin, Dan, Gad, Issachar, Joseph, Judah, Levi, Naphtali, Reuben, Simeon, Zebulon

Thus saith the Lord GOD; This [shall be] the border, whereby ye shall inherit the land according to the twelve tribes of Israel: Joseph [shall have two] portions. Eze 47:13

Of course, all the Tribes are important, but the ones we are most concerned with, are the two sons of Joseph, Ephraim and Manasseh, and the Tribe of Judah, or the Jews, as this is the tribe from which the Messiah would be born. He was a descendant of King David.

The twelve tribes had argued among themselves and the nation of Israel was split. It had become two nations, the nation of Israel and the nation of Judah. Israel in the north had Solomon as their King, while Judah in the South had King Rehoboam.

> **But [as for] the children of Israel which dwelt in the cities of Judah, Rehoboam reigned over them. 1Ki 12:17**

So, some years later when Babylon invaded and defeated Israel, it was only ten tribes that were taken into captivity. King Solomon's Temple was destroyed and looted; this is when the Ark of the Covenant with the Ten Commandants inside disappeared. It was never known if the Babylonians took the Ark with them or if the Priest managed to hide the ark in the catacombs below the Temple, or if they managed to smuggle it out of Israel entirely. The Ark of the Covenant has not been seen since.

The legend that surrounded the Ark kept it in the realm of mysteries. The Ark could not be touched with the bare hand, to do so would bring immediate death. The Ark could only be handled with rods placed in the holders on each side of the Ark just for that purpose. The army that marched into battle carrying the Ark before it was invincible. The Ark was kept in the most *Holy of Holies,* behind the velvet curtain at the back of the temple. Only the Levi priests had access to it and only on holy days did the priest ever enter the most *Holy of Holies.*

So the tribes of Judah and Levi were all that remained of the nation of Israel. The Ten lost Tribes never returned to their homeland, as they had done once before when taken into captivity. To all accounts and purposes, history lost them; they lost their identity, they became part of their captors' lives, at first they were slaves, then later they married into their captors' families losing themselves even more.

But you can trace where the Lost Tribes ended up by researching where their captors migrated to over the next thousand years. They are there, and later I will reveal where Ephraim and Manasseh settled and what nations they are today. This has very much to do with the redemption of Man.

Although the nation of Israel had sinned against their God, God still intended to keep the promise He made to Abraham centuries before, for it was an unconditional promise, and that promise has been fulfilled.

Ephraim became many nations and even to this day, still is a power to reckon with and is the nation of Great Britain. Plus, the throne of England is the throne of King David. David was promised that there would be no end to his kingdom, even to the end of time. When Christ returns to Earth, it is this throne he will rightfully claim.

Manasseh became one great nation, today it is the only remaining super power, the United States of America.

When Mary and Joseph, both descendents of King David, were married, Mary was already pregnant with the Holy Seed. Gabriel had visited the young girl, she was all of fifteen and told her she was blessed among women, for she would conceive a child, and his name would be Jesus, that he would inherit the throne of his father, King David and to his kingdom, there would be no end.

The child was born in a stable, a very humble beginning for a King, a Messiah. King Herod, when he learned from the three wise men from the East of the birth of a new king, sent out his soldiers and ordered all male children under the age of two to be killed. Satan was trying to do away with the Messiah before he could give himself in sacrifice for the redemption of Man.

To murder him as a child was not what was required. It must be done with knowledge and with willingness. Satan tried many times in the life of Jesus to either lead him into temptation or even kill him outright before his time.

But Christ had a league of angels always at his side to protect him until the appointed time with the cross. After the trial and judgment was passed on Jesus, and he was hanging on the cross, Christ felt it when God redrew his hand of protection and removed the angels from their appointed post, so that the Son of Man could be slaughtered as a Lamb for the Sacrifice. Had the angels remained with Christ he could not have been captured and crucified.

Christ cried, **"My God, My God, why have you forsaken Me?"** and gave up the Ghost, or his Spirit, which every human has.

By now, the skies were black, thunder rolled, and the heavy curtain in the temple that protected the Holy of Holies, ripped from top to bottom. It was not yet evening yet darkness covered the land, graves were opened and the dead walked the Earth.

And the graves were opened; and many bodies of the saints which slept arose, Matthew 27:52

This took place on a holy day, the Passover, which was on a Wednesday afternoon. As was customary with the Jews' religious customs, they could not handle an unclean thing on the Sabbath, which began after sunset and a dead body was the most unclean thing there was. There was no time to cleanse the body of blood and anoint it with oil; they only had time to put a shroud about the body and to lay it in a rock tomb.

As the Passover occurred over several days, Wednesday eve thru Friday eve and then the real Sabbath, the eve on Saturday thru morning on Sunday which made three nights and three days, no one could touch the body until after sunrise Sunday Morning. So a heavy boulder was placed in front of the tomb and Pilate ordered two Roman soldiers to guard the tomb.

Sunday morning, early, Mary Magdalene hurried to the tomb so that she could properly dress the body for burial. She was alone and she intended to have the guards roll the heavy stone away from the tomb's entrance so that she could enter the tomb.

But when she arrived, there was an earthquake and an angel rolled away the stone, the angel spoke to them saying, ***"I know you have come for Jesus, but he is not here. He is risen as he said." Matthew chapter 28.***

Christ remained on the Earth for another forty days, then he was taken up into Heaven and an angel appeared saying that He would return in like manner.

Chapter Four

You know how sometimes when you are looking forward to an event, how it seems to take such a long time? So long, in fact, that you think it is never going to happen. Well the return of Christ to this Earth is like that. Two thousand years have passed with each generation thinking his return is imminent but at last they die and still things go on, and still true followers of Christ look for his return. Just remember, the minute you let down your guard, that is when the sun rises and daylight fills the Earth and our Lord has touched down on the Mount of Olives. No, it hasn't happened yet, but continue with your vigil, for as the Bible tells us, he will come as a thief in the night.

My life today is pretty easy going, just doing the same mundane chores day after day, I talk with at least one of my sisters every week, and we exchange the gossip that goes on in every family. Nothing too exciting happening with our sons and daughters or grand children and that's good, I enjoy the peace that a boring day can bring.

Then one day, as I was watching the evening news, the report was that there had been more suicide attacks in Israel and Hamas was behind it. This time instead of the Israeli government sending more troops into Palatine, they went into Jerusalem and placed forces around the Dome of the Rock, holding it hostage.

The pictures being shown were of Israelis also coming to this Place of Worship to reinforce the government troops there. The Jehamic community also arrived at the Place of Worship but all the Religious Groups were forced out of the shrine, and so we were at a standoff.

The phone rings, picking it up I greet my sister Anne, "Hey, what's up?"

"Are you watching the news?" Anne asks.

"As a matter of fact I am. You know the Dome of the Rock is one of the most holy shrines there is to Jeham, next to Sodeem."

"They're killing people. Some of them are so stupid as to walk right up to the outer part where soldiers have the thing surrounded. It's mighty bloody. I'm surprised that they are showing this mess on television."

"I know, it is disturbing but I can't keep my eyes off of it. I'm watching Coxx, who are you watching?" I asked. I liked 'the all news channels' for my world news and my local channels for local and state news.

"I'm on channel eleven, I don't have satellite any more so I can't get the channels you can."

My sister Anne occasionally would run into financial problems and cut back on some things, then things would pick up and she would get them back. 'But that was life,' she said.

We spoke on for a few more minutes and then said 'goodbye.'

The next few days at home, we went through our day-to-day routine, I was complaining more and more about how much my right knee was hurting and thinking about whether I should go back to Dr. Rosenbloom and have knee surgery.

Thomas had had a colonoscopy done and three polyps were found and removed, the doctor told us they would be tested for cancer and the results sent to us. If they turned out to be cancerous, then Thomas would need to have this test done again in three years instead of five.

Next year I most likely will begin this same type of screening as part of my yearly physical examination.

The world news was constantly on the story surrounding the Dome of the Rock and the standoff there. The Israeli government was reported to be sending in archeologists but when asked about this they would only say they were checking out the catacombs below the Place of Worship. No further details were given. Outside the Place of Worship, Jeham was threatening more suicide attacks if Israel did not vacate the Dome of the Rock.

The avian flu had now spread into Europe with sporadic outbreaks and a vaccine still months away and with not nearly enough. It would be given to the most vulnerable people first. It was also being reported that tuberculosis was making a return and was highly resistant to the antibiotic used normally to treat and cure it. Mumps, a common childhood disease was also returning in a mutated state so that the vaccination given to prevent it offered only minimal protection, if any. These diseases were being reported in my home state of North Carolina, which was bringing world news a little too close to home.

Our weather has been strange for several years now, there was hurricane Fran, that hit North Carolina in 1996 and we had some damage from it. Then Floyd in 2000 that flooded most of North Carolina, leaving hundreds dead, and so much damage that we are still repairing and rebuilding our state. Although spared being flooded ourselves by mere feet, our well water was contaminated and is just now returning to its pre-flood condition.

And now spring storms coming across the country are furious and dangerous, destroying thousands of miles of countryside, leaving many dead and homeless, this after the New Orleans' disaster of last year, from which the nation is still reeling.

The latest spring storm has spawned hundreds of tornadoes in the Midwest as far east as Tennessee and hundreds of families are now homeless, adding to the count from the Katrina disaster of last year.

Larraine called, "Hey, just letting you know that we are okay."

"Yeah, I saw it on the morning news; north and east of you were hard hit!"

"We just dodged the bullet," she continued and I could hear the least bit of fright in her voice. "I haven't been this scared of a storm since Floyd flooded North Carolina. We left the trailer and stayed the night with our landlord in their house. She even let me bring my children."

I laughed, Larraine referred to her five cats, and three dogs as 'my children.'

"That was real nice of her; at least you know where you can go the next time storms like that come through your area."

"Tennessee was hard hit," she went on, "ten people died there."

"Yeah, I heard and now they are heading our way. But they are supposed to lose their punch by the time they get here, I sure hope so."

We spoke on for a few more minutes when my call-waiting beeped in, it was Clara, I told Larraine who it was and that I would check in with her later to let her know how we came through these very violent storms.

"Morning, Clara, what's up?"

"Alice, I can't get Larraine on the phone and she is not online!" Clara obviously was concerned about our sister in Texas.

"Not to worry, I was talking to her when you called."

"Oh good," she said with an audible sigh. "How is she?"

I related that all was fine. There was some damage from inch-sized hail but that was all.

Today the *Today's News* reports that the United States is planning a nuclear attack on Iran. Just how true this is, is anybody's guess. I would like to think that my country would not consider using these weapons without plausible cause. Just suspecting that Iran is trying to develop weapons of mass destruction is not enough, there must be concrete evidence.

The standoff at the Dome of the Rock continues into its third week and just now nothing more has happened but plans are being made by both sides on how to end it.

I go about my chores with the TV running and as I am sitting, folding clothes while watching *Roland and Faith*, a news alert breaks in.

'We interrupt your regular programming to bring you this latest out of Jerusalem. Let's go to our news reporter, on the scene, live via satellite.'

I continue following the news story by changing the channel to Coxx because I know they will stay with the story longer than any of the regular networks.

The Coxx reporter is in the middle of his report as I tune in, the scene is chaotic and there is debris and smoke in large clouds over the city as the reporter continues with his report... "A massive earthquake beneath the *Dome of the Rock* occurred just under an hour ago. It happened at just about the time that a large crowd of Religious Groups was marching in protest towards the Place of Worship. These protests have been going on for weeks as you know but no attempt to approach the Dome was tried until today. As the Israeli soldiers were preparing to repel the advance of the thousands of Jehamic protestors, the ground began to shake. This stopped the march of the protesters as they turned and ran from the Dome. They were closely followed by the Israeli soldiers also attempting to escape the quake."

The coverage continued into the day but information as to what happened exactly was slow in being revealed. The Jerusalem quake happened around 9:30 AM my time and as nothing new was being reported I put on a DVD to watch and to clear my thoughts.

When I did return to the regular networks I was surprised that the local station obviously was still covering the quake, but wait, no, this was another earthquake.

"Another quake?" I asked myself. It was 2:30 in the afternoon, almost time to pick Lexis up at school. "Where is this one?"

The information at first was confusing since I was coming in during the middle of the reporting and it was several minutes before updates were released.

"If you are just tuning in, you might assume we are still covering the earthquake in Jerusalem but that is not the case. This quake is on the other side of the world, San Francisco in fact."

The reporter this time was female and obviously trying hard to hold her emotions in check and give her viewers an unbiased account of what was known about this latest disaster.

Since this one happened in the United States, there was more information immediately known, it was a 9.7 on the Richter scale with the epic-center ten miles east of the city. It happened at 11:00AM local time an hour before the noon time rush hour, which had thousands still in business buildings resulting in more casualties than otherwise might have happened.

Most new construction in San Francisco was built to withstand a 7.7 quake but the 9.7 was too much and although many buildings remained standing long enough for the occupants to evacuate they were now starting to collapse much like the twin towers did in Manhattan on 9/11/2001.

As with Jerusalem, it was nothing but confusion as rescue workers were beginning to come onto different disaster scenes. I left to pick up Lexis; she was all excited when she began telling me about the two earthquakes.

"Grandma," her anxiety level was high and she spoke too loudly and too fast, "there were two earthquakes today, did you know that?"

"Yes Lexis, I heard. Do you know where they were?"

"One was over in Iraq ..."

I stopped her, "No, it wasn't in Iraq; it was in the country of Israel, the city of Jerusalem. You remember where the Religious Groups were protesting at the Place of Worship there?"

"Oh, I thought they were fighting in Baghdad."

I filled her in with accurate details as best as I could, I wasn't feeling as calm as I sounded for this definitely had me very upset.

Things went from bad to worse at both disaster zones as in the next few days we learned of thousands killed at each site. The earthquake in Jerusalem was the most baffling of either, as it is not prone to earthquakes and scientists were searching to find a fault line there but nothing was revealed.

Every single person inside of the Place of Worship at the time of the earthquake was killed, for the Dome itself remained in one piece and just crushed the ground beneath it, flattening the supporting walls.

But not only did Jeham lose a shrine but so did the Jews, for the *Wailing Wall*, the last remaining part of the Temple still standing after the Romans destroyed the Temple in 79 AD, also collapsed with not a brick left upon another. Every one praying at the wall died, it was not understood why, because the wall did not collapse on them and it was speculated that the majority of them died from the dust created from the exploding bricks as they crumbled to dust, suffocating the worshippers.

The thought sent chills through me and I became more and more tied to the news channels trying to learn everything I could. If I had heard everything on one channel and they were starting to repeat themselves, I would tune to another channel and would generally learn something different on that one.

Thomas told me I was getting obsessed and I needed to leave it for a while. But, like the pictures after 9/11, these scenes of horror and disaster were upsetting but, nevertheless, compelling to watch.

I watched as bodies were pulled from the rubble, some were still alive but mostly, they were dead. The most heartbreaking of all were the children. Some were seen sitting in the middle of streets crying, mere infants some of them, while people ran past them trying to get out of danger.

And so, we begin.....

Chapter Five

Another week of this, switching from disaster scene to disaster scene, and I was beginning to get the two mixed up. We now had totals of how many casualties there were and an estimate of dollar damage. The toll for the dead and injured at the Place of Worship was 233 with another 2,012 around the wall and surrounding area. It was closer to 26,000 in San Francisco.

The search for survivors ended and removal of debris from both zones began and the talk of reconstruction. The all news' channels began covering other news and only reported on the progress of these two sites in regular news slots. In the United States, FEMA had redeemed itself somewhat by being on top of the disaster within hours of the event.

As usual whenever a disaster hit, fund-raising started, for both parts of the world.

In Israel, more Israelis were killed than the Religious Groups, which led to the Jehamic world shouting for the destruction of Israel and implying that the earthquake was Allah's way of punishing the infidels for the desecration of holy ground.

Oddly enough, the terrorists that were fighting in Iraq were migrating towards Israel. Israel called up their reserves and activated their form of a national draft, which led to speculation of an all-out assault on

Israel. The United States also called up their reserves and canceled all leaves.

Reinforcements arrived at the Dome of the Rock, which now included US and British military forces. The Jehamic extremists seethed with anger at this, and reaffirmed their Jihad on the West.

At home, the terrorist level went as high as red and stayed. Of course, the price of gasoline went past four dollars a gallon. This meant that Lexis had to start riding the school bus instead of me taking her. I had no choice really, for gasoline was now being rationed and only one car per family could be filled up every two weeks.

Thankfully, neither Thomas nor I had to drive to work and so we didn't suffer like some others. Art, who ran his own construction business was finding it hard to find work and really needed to go out of town in search of jobs.

Thomas and I would siphon the gas out of my car and give it to Art for his work truck, and Lance was learning to stay home, or walk, or ride a bike where he needed to go, saving his allotment of gasoline for transportation to work. The government issued gas-rationing cards that worked much like debit or credit cards. This brought about a new demand, and thefts of these cards, which were worth more on the black market than stolen credit cards.

Naturally, with gas being so high, the price of other commodities was also rising, fresh produce and meats were beginning to disappear from store shelves, with their canned counterparts now the only things you could buy. This occurred over a period of months and kind of sneaked up on you. One week, you could buy fresh milk, bread, eggs, vegetables, and meats and the next, you couldn't, with only canned or dried products available.

Saudi Arabia sought a summit with the West, the Prime Minister of Britain, the President of the United States, Prime Minister of Japan, of Spain and a few others, all arriving at the United Nations building in New York for this secret summit. Of course, the media speculated at what the Saudis wanted but it was ever such a shock when it came out a few days later.

It seems that the Jehamic community wanted the Dome that still sat upon the rubble at the Temple Mound. There was a deal offered, for Israel to allow for its removal and the Religious Groups to give up claim to the site on which the Dome of the Rock sat.

The Religious Groups now felt that the site was unclean with the dead of Jews still buried beneath the Dome.

Seven days later, the Israeli government agreed, as long as it was the United States that conducted its removal. This point brought on more arguments, for the Saudis did not want the infidels to touch the holy relic, and so talks continued a little longer. It was finally agreed that the United Arab Emirates would be the ones to do the actual removal and the United States would oversee and provide security.

I thought just how much of a fabrication this was, for it was the United States that would provide the equipment for this operation.

We had a sisters' get-together at my house. All but Larraine would come, she lived in Texas but we would call her on the phone and we would share our thoughts.

Anne arrived first, "Hey Alice. I'm first, I see."

"Yes, but Clara should be here any minute. Hey Wayne, come on in. Thomas is in the living room watching TV."

"Alice!"

Clara was coming in the back door. Everyone had brought something for our dinner. I had cooked a turkey with all the trimmings. Clara brought paper plates and cups, and Anne had made potato salad and homemade sweet tea.

We no longer had the children at our get-togethers, for they were grown now with their own families and there were just too many of them to get into my small house, so just the sisters got together on special days and sometimes for no reason at all. Today was Easter, and this was the first Easter we would have congregated here for this holiday.

Easter egg hunts were being held at our grown children's houses and Thomas had taken Lexis to Art's house for theirs.

I had two grandchildren by Art and Kerry, a six year old girl, Brook, who was in the first grade and my only granddaughter, and Little Art, or as his parents called him, Mini-Man who was four.

Lance had one son by a woman much older than he, she had two other children, girls, Bryce was her only boy, and he was now three. Most likely, I would see all of them later on in the day.

But for now, it was just Anne and Wayne, Clara, Thomas, and I for Easter dinner.

We chatted idly over our meal, "I don't see how much more gas prices can go up. Even though we are allowed to fill up every two weeks, a tank of gas for my Mazda was sixty-three dollars Friday. If Art gets this tank, like he has the others, he's going to have to pay me for it," I shook my head as I spoke. "I can't afford to give that much money away every month. I can do it every once in awhile but..."

"I know, I made it here for this get-together but next time y'all are going to have to come to my house," declared Clara.

"I don't even take Lexis to school. The only place I go is Wal-Mart every other week and my doctor. And with groceries going up in price along with gas, it's got to the point that I hate shopping."

"I told Darlene that same thing. I think she thinks money grows on trees," sighed Anne. "I will be so glad when she begins thinking more clearly than she does. She's got three kids. I can't, and Wayne wouldn't let me anyway, take those children to raise."

"Well, you are lucky you have only one like that and she'll get better now that you have told her so and if you stick to it," I said.

"I've got to, Alice. I want some free time for Wayne and myself. You remember how Mama used to say, 'I don't have any small children.' Well, that's my motto from now on. It's time they learned how to take care of themselves!"

Thomas sat and ate without saying much of anything, which is normal for him, he's not much for idle talk, and he asked Wayne, "Wanna ride down the road with me? I thought I'd go to Pittman's Junk yard to find parts for that Jeep I'm working on."

"Sure, but are they open on Easter?" asked Wayne.

"Not to the public, but he is a friend and said I could come by anytime to just give him a call," explained Thomas.

So we girls were left to clear the table and clean up. Afterwards, we decided to go outside and sit in the swings out under the water oaks in the back yard.

It was spring and the weather was so pretty that it was really nice to linger in the shade.

"Alice, did you hear how the satellite took pictures of that mountain?" asked Anne.

"Are you talking about the image that looked like a giant boat," I replied. "They've sent an expedition there to see if it might be Noah's Ark."

"Yeah, that one. Have you heard anything about it lately?"

"The last thing I heard was that they were at the site and that it is indeed a wooden boat. They sent some of the members of the expedition back with samples of the wood to analyze and carbon date but I haven't heard anything else. Have you?"

"No, I know you watch the news more than I do and was just wondering. Do you think they can prove it is Noah's Ark?"

"Several things are in its favor, for one, its location. On a mountain top? You don't normally find boats on mountains."

At that remark everyone laughed, "I know what it would do for Christians," said Clara.

"Yeah, it would be like finding the Holy Grail," said Anne.

"Or the lost Ark with the ten Commandments," I inserted.

"It would prove there is a God," said Clara.

We all were silent for a moment, then quite suddenly the wind picked up and it was obvious that a spring storm was brewing. A few minutes later, large raindrops began falling as thunder cracked and a bolt of lightning streaked across the sky over our heads. Then the sky opened up and before we could get inside, we were drenched. Everyone ran, or in my case, hobbled to the back door, Anne and Clara almost dragged me inside while Thomas held the door open.

"I hope I never have to run for my life," I said, "because I sure wouldn't make it."

"Wow!" declared Clara, "Where did that come from?"

"It's spring," said Anne, "Storms can come up real quick you know."

"Let's see what's on the weather channel," I suggested as I led everyone into the living room to where the TV was.

Sitting around, we gazed at the TV as I tuned in the weather channel on 64. The news was good and this shower wouldn't last long, to which Clara said, "I'll wait until the heaviest part is gone, then I've got to go."

I tuned to the Coxx channel for the news to play in the background as we continued with our conversation.

"I'm worried about my job," said Clara. "We are having trouble with my people getting to work. They are complaining about working for minimal wage with gas so high. They have to work three quarters of an hour for just a gallon of gas. Some have already quit and the others want a cost of living raise. I've asked Mr. Majors about giving them eight dollars an hour but he said to wait it out, that the prices are bound to go down. Meanwhile, I have to do the work of those that quit and I ain't liking that a bit."

"Hush!" Clara shouted.

We looked at her as if she was crazy.

"What is it," asked Anne.

"The television!" she replied as she pointed toward the screen.

"...dating for the wood proves it to be from the time of the Biblical story of Noah and the flood. This of course does not prove it is Noah's Ark only that it is from that period. There is only one way for a ship of that size to be where it is and that is for it to have floated there."

The reporter continued with his story, "...and what will this discovery mean not only to Christians, but to Jews and Religious Groups as well."

"That settles it for me," said Clara. "That proves that the great flood happened and if that happened as the Bible said, then there really is a 'God'!"

Chapter Six

Yes, this new information about the ship found on Mount Ararat in Turkey that summer, was constantly being discussed on all the news' channels. The tragedies of the two earthquakes began to fade and now took a backseat to this new unbelievable discovery!

Things were starting to happen really fast now; the United States' President was under such tremendous pressure to find a solution to the gasoline crisis that he invoked his war time privileges and ordered that oil be searched for in the Alaskan National Parks, as well as any other government-owned lands that might produce the black gold.

He opened up the government reserves, which helped somewhat and gave the nation time to search for new oil fields on US soil. Desperate times called for desperate measures and a freeze was placed on the price of gasoline at the pumps.

This didn't go over well with the large oil companies but there was not a thing they could do. Gasoline was frozen at $4.75 a gallon, just $1.25 short of minimum wage. The rationing continued and demonstrations became more prevalent and violent.

The Teamsters for the trucking industry called for a strike, demanding special privileges for truckers so that once again commodities could be trucked less expensively across the nation. They had lots of support, for everyone wanted their former merchandise back in the stores.

Dairy farmers were pouring fresh milk out into the streets in protest at the high cost of getting their product to market. Many other cultivators followed suit or simply refused to plant at all. Now there was no work for the migrant workers, many of whom were here illegally from Mexico. They were seeking aid from our Social Services, overwhelming them to the point that many were turning away applicants, if they did not at least have a green card.

The flow of illegal immigrants coming across the Mexican border was cut by two thirds; there simply was no reason for them to come. There were no jobs!

Martial law came into effect to stifle the wide spread demonstrations and to stop looting of closed grocery stores. The nation as a whole had a nine o'clock curfew.

Yes, it was getting bad; the power companies began rationing electricity, if you can imagine that. The power load was lowered so that only a minimum of household appliances could run at any one time. Candles were once again in demand and not as just an accent but as a necessity. You watched television by candlelight, which was an old Abe Lincoln joke but now had real meaning. Whenever possible you conserved electricity.

All of this happened because of the price of oil, which by the way was now $109.00 a barrel. OPEC had a stranglehold on the United States economy.

In Israel, the Dome had been successfully removed from the site and taken to Saudi Arabia. It had been an ordeal for the country, and there had been instances of violence at the site. These were mostly Religious Groups' protesters who did not want the Dome removed but instead a new Place of Worship built on the spot. After the Dome left Israel, the government started arresting any non-citizens at the site and either deporting them or keeping them in jail, if any were wanted by the government.

The very day after the Dome's removal, emergency workers began cleaning the site of debris, and of course, there were the remains of those killed inside of the Place of Worship. The stench must have been horrific, for the workers were actually wearing gas masks!

"Now for the latest from Iran," the reporter continued. "There are rumors from intelligence sources reporting that Iran has developed the bomb. They deny it. The United Nations is requesting that inspectors be allowed back into the country to verify their claim."

"Thomas, this is scaring me," I said as we were both sitting here watching the evening news on Coxx. I hardly watched any other news' networks now, for the reports that they gave were without concern, as though this was only a bother and nothing would come of it. I wasn't all that sure.

"Well, I think we need to be worried. We know that countries like that will use it."

"Their most likely target will be Israel. That country is surrounded by Jehamic nations that would do almost anything to get rid of them, even risking exposure to radiation for themselves. I would think or hope they would really think about nuclear exchange because Israel has had the bomb for a long while. And their defenses are even better than ours. The first sign of missiles being launched would trigger them to fire theirs and it would be over for that part of world."

"I don't think they would use missiles," replied Thomas.

"You don't?"

"No, what they would do is have a bomb carried in, maybe on a truck or by a suicide bomber."

"Uumm, a truck maybe, I would think a nuclear bomb would be too large for any one person to carry in." We were both speculating, for there was no way we as laypersons would know how to deliver a weapon such as this, without a lot of noticeable activity. There were spies everywhere, especially in the sky.

"Even if they have made the bomb," continued Thomas, "To be sure they would be too smart to use it."

"That's where you are wrong, Thomas," I argued. "These extremist believe if they killed an infidel at the same time they are killing themselves, that there will be seventy virgins waiting for them in Paradise. They do not mind dying for their beliefs. In the Jehamic religion, to be a martyr is something great!"

"But they are committing suicide," he protested. "Isn't that the unforgivable sin?"

"For a Christian it is but I don't know about Jeham, like I said if they are also killing the infidel when they die, they will be rewarded. But I don't know what the women suicide bombers' reward in Paradise would be, seems a little lopsided to me!"

A week later, first thing in the morning while watching our local stations for the news and weather, they began to report, "Out of Israel this morning, while you slept, something was unearthed from the catacombs beneath the Temple Mound. While trying to inspect it, three Israeli soldiers were struck dead after merely touching the object.

"The site was evacuated and specialists sent in, geared up in what can only be described as hazard suits. Speculations are that a nuclear weapon had been found beneath the place of worship and must have been hidden there somehow by the Religious Groups. There is a lot of conjecture as to how this could have been done or how long it might have been hidden there.

"We have new reports," said the male news reporter as from one side of the screen a paper was handed to him. "Excuse me folks for a moment," and he took a few seconds to read the document then looked at the camera again, "We now have video by way of satellite from the Temple Mound in Jerusalem."

He continued speaking as pictures of the activity were shown. We saw several ambulances and then more military equipment, tanks and Humvees and two helicopters.

"The United States and Britain, who have been here since the earthquake, are helping with the recovery of this object.

We go live now to Jerusalem where George Chapman has arrived on the scene only moments ago.

George, what can you tell us?"

George Chapman of Good Morning USA now speaks, "Good morning, so far we are not being told anything and we were asked to do our reporting from the roof of the Marriot here in Jerusalem. Our cameraman is only able to record with a telescopic lens, so I am afraid the picture quality is very poor. It will be dark here in three hours and they want to have this object out before then."

The news then was a repeat of what they already knew, so I turned to the Coxx channel as I went about my chores. Thomas went outside to his garage to work on a van for Harry Joyner, a friend and now a customer. Thomas had taken up car repair on the side since his retirement. It really was a big help now what with a fixed income and prices soaring as they have been over the past eighteen months.

Nothing new was reported all day, so mid-afternoon, Thomas and I settled back in our recliners in the living room for an afternoon nap, before Lexis would get home from school at about three forty five in the afternoon.

The TV was on but on the Western Channel. Naps are better when taken to the sounds of a low playing boring movie. Upon awakening, I wanted to find out what was going on in Israel and Thomas changed the channel when I asked.

It was on Coxx, and it was Chamber I with Carl Jones reporting.

"...they are coming out with the object now," he was saying.

There was a live video feed but still at a distance, so all we could see were the military and rescue vehicles and men in uniform going about outside the pile of rubble of what was once the Dome of the Rock Place of Worship.

"It seems," said Jones, "that this object is considered very dangerous. A carrier of sorts has been constructed around the object, as everyone is afraid to touch it. After all, three men died when they did.

I find it hard to describe the atmosphere in Israel around this site. To say it is solemn would be understating it. We were told a few minutes ago that several Rabbis have now gone into the catacombs, which will lead you to believe this is not a nuclear weapon but perhaps something of a religious nature.

When the Temple stood there, it was a well known fact that these tunnels were below the Temple. It was believed that the Priest would often hide valuables there during a time of crisis, wait, there's something...

Yes, they are emerging now from the opening that leads down into the catacombs."

As Carl Jones continued talking, Thomas and I were focused on the screen. A few soldiers emerged first and marched as if at attention, as though leading a procession, with their rifles held rigidly on their shoulders.

Next came two men, but, oddly, they were dressed in white robes with some sort of headdress.

"Thomas," I began.

Now they were completely outside, there were four men total, in white robes, and they were carrying a large box-shaped object that was completely covered with a violet velvet cover. There were two long poles at the base of this box and this is what the men were holding. The top of the box was not flat but was irregularly shaped in two peaks. Four more soldiers followed, these were American and British.

"Oh my God," I almost screamed, for it was clear to me what they had.

Thomas looked at me, "What is it?"

"Thomas, that's the Lost Ark of the Covenant!"

Now Thomas was looking at me as if I was a crazed woman, "What is that?"

"The Ark that holds the Ten Commandants! The one that was lost when Babylon invaded Israel and took the ten tribes into captivity, and neither were ever seen again."

"Ladies and gentlemen," Carl was now saying, "It is being reported that what they have is the Lost Ark of the Covenant containing the Ten Commandants!

"There is a news conference scheduled for seven o'clock eastern time."

The time in Israel was nine hours ahead of us so three o'clock PM for us, meant it was twelve o'clock there; the news conference was four hours away, four AM for Israel.

The news conference was ready to begin. I had spent the afternoon on the phone talking with every one of my sisters as well as a few friends about this latest discovery and to make sure that everyone was watching this news conference.

"Yes, this is the Ark of the Covenant. It has been taken to a synagogue for its protection and a holy site for the worship of Yahweh. As we were unable to keep the location completely secret the synagogue is surrounded by armed guards. This is not only for the protection of the Ark but also those who might be curious. The Ark is deadly should it be touched by anyone but a high Priest from the Tribe of Levi and even they cannot touch it except during Holy Days. Thus, the Ark has not been opened to see whether the Ten Commandants are still inside.

"We believe that the earthquake is responsible for the uncovering of the Ark. There is evidence at the site where the Ark rested, that it was buried in solid rock, this could not have been done by mere humans. We believe that it was supernaturally concealed by the Hand of God.

"We also believe that this earthquake was also supernaturally started as it was time for the Ark to be given back to Israel in our time of need.

"Whoever ever carries the Ark into battle is invincible. Yahweh once again has favored his chosen people with His presence.

"Plans for the building of a new Temple in this location are already being planned. May Yahweh's blessings be upon us."

Chapter Seven

The news that two legends of the Bible had been found set the religious community on its ear. Debates were widespread; everyone wanted proof or access to these relics, Religious Groups and Christians alike. But Israel was in charge of the Ark of the Covenant and they were being very zealous in guarding it from the rest of the world.

The site where King Solomon's Temple once stood would once again support a Jewish Temple.

The world watched in fascination as this temple went up in about one and one half years' time. It was beautiful and was as regal as King Solomon's Temple, for it was built to the exact specification of that one. Its designs are laid out in the Bible. Begin reading at **(1Kings 6:15)**

Once so sacred to the Jews, the Wailing Wall, or what was left of it after the earthquake, was torn down so that the new temple could be built upon that ground. The stones were crushed and mixed in with new building material for the new temple.

The last year went by in a blur, with so much happening in the world that it was hard to keep track of it all. These Christian/Jewish/Religious Groups' religious artifacts brought many people back into the Churches/Synagogues/Places of Worship the world over. But to which religion should the artifacts (for want of a better word) belong? Judaism insisted that since theirs was the oldest of the three and they were the original chosen people, that rightfully it was theirs. I would tend to agree on that, only, both Christian and Religious Groups also claimed the same heritage as the Jews. So the debate continued. It seemed no one could agree, which was nothing new.

During the reign of Chancellor Jude First, there had been communications with the rulers in Israel and after some fifty odd years, the Asbathian Principal Church apologized to the Jews for the holocaust of World War II. There had been talk of the Chancellor visiting Israel but the late Chancellor was just too ill for such a trip.

During the year, Noah's Ark had been removed from Mount Ararat. It had been a long tedious job, but with large investors interested in this true artifact, the work took more than a couple of years to complete. Not wanting to cut or dismantle the vessel, and with it being too large to be flown off the mountain, they had undertaken the task of building a road down the mountain side. Tunnels had been cut into the virgin rock and the road wound through the mountain and around its steep sides. The Ark was then taken under cover of night to yet another secret location, but remained in Turkey.

Reports on it came out only a few weeks ago.

The scientists working on Noah's Ark gave a news conference.

"Good evening everyone. I know you are all anxious for our report on the finding and evaluation of this vessel, so I'll get on with it."

The speaker was a man in his late thirties and dressed in a light colored business suit. Two armed men in unfamiliar military uniforms stood behind and on each side of him. He stood on a podium, which held many microphones.

"We cleaned her up as best we could without damaging the delicate lumber.

We have had a great deal of difficulty identifying the lumber used. We know that the Old Testament tells us that the ark was made of Gopher wood. Well there is no known tree by that name. We eliminated cypress, pine, cedar, fir, juniper, and many others that grew in the regions at that time. We must remember that if the flood did indeed occur that we would be foolish to think that all species survived. This tree from which the lumber came is extinct.

But everything else matches what we know about the Ark from the description from Genesis chapter six, verse fourteen forward.

We must also remember the measurements were in 'cubits' which is not a precise unit of measure. Each period in history that used 'cubit' as a measurement had different ways of doing so. Generally, it was measured from the tip of the thumb, or another finger such as the third finger for it is the longest digit, to the elbow. This is roughly forty-five centimeters or eighteen inches for the average man.

Thus the length of three hundred cubits would be four hundred and fifty feet.

Its width of fifty cubits would be seventy-five feet.

Its height of thirty cubits would be forty-five feet.

Whilst our measurements are not exactly those, they are close enough to say that these measurements match.

The vessel has three floors, not counting what we would call a deck. It has no deck but a window at the top level and a large door beneath that. We would assume this was the main and only entrance into the Ark by both beast and man. Also, all around the vessel are what can only be called 'port-holes'. They are quite small, about the size of a man's face."

"Most likely these were used for ventilation and for viewing.

Below deck, there are many rooms, or shall we say stalls, for they are sectioned off but not enclosed.

We are continuing research and examination of the vessel but I think we can say with a certain amount of conviction that this is indeed the famed Noah's Ark.

I thank you for your time and now I and my colleagues will take a few questions."

This news conference was continued and shown repeatedly on all networks. The Chancellor asked for permission to visit Noah's Ark and surprisingly he also wanted to visit the newly built temple in Jerusalem.

Talks were underway between Israel, the Turkish government, and the Goveian for these visits. The Chancellor wanted these two visits in one trip.

During the past year, gas prices had actually come down and so the government lifted the freeze and prices stabilized at $3.10 a gallon, not cheap but better. Oil had been discovered in one of Alaska's national parks; drilling began immediately, and soon the new supply was added to the oil already heading down the Alaskan pipeline.

In Iraq, we actually had our troops to come home, leaving only training troops to continue teaching the Iraqi military. Electricity was once more abundant enough and we were back to our normal level of usage. Elections held in the following year, saw a Democrat back in the White House, no surprise there. Reluctantly, I voted. Most people were disillusioned and many stayed away from the polls in protest, and so we now had a woman President. Oh well, to be sure she couldn't do worse than any of the men who had held this high office.

So, the world looked as if it might be returning to normal, but nothing was further from the truth. The country heaved a sigh of relief that we were no longer fighting a full scale war in Iraq.

Al Qaeda was not defeated, only gone underground, no matter that Osama Bin Laden had finally been killed; there was always another ready to step in to replace him. But losing the Al Qaeda leader did remove a large financial support for the terrorist group, which was probably one reason they disappeared. But were they really gone? Or, were they only regrouping? There were ways of finding out and, hopefully, that is just what our Intelligence Services were doing.

I heard my name called and knew my sister, Anne, had dropped by for a visit. It was about four o'clock in the afternoon and she had just picked up her husband from work and stopped by on her way home. Wayne headed for the garage where Thomas was and Anne and I sat outside in the swing. It was late October, with fall being my favorite season.

The breezes were gentle as they swept the fallen leaves into small dirt devils, which one of my cats began chasing across the yard.

"What's you and Wayne been up to?" I asked.

We discussed everyday problems, our grown kids of course and the grand children and the news her son Michael and his wife were expecting their first child. Michael was Anne's youngest child and only son. He had married a year ago and now his family would start next April.

We then drifted to the subject of the Lost Ark of the Covenant and the finding of Noah's Ark.

"I think the finding of these two religious symbols means something, don't you?" I asked.

"You know, I have been thinking on it a lot lately..." Anne said.

"Yeah, me too," I interrupted.

"Great minds think alike," she laughed. "Do you think that God had a hand in letting Noah's Ark and the Ark of Moses be found?"

"Yes, people have looked for over two thousand years for the Ark that holds the Ten Commandants," I said. "They have done TV shows about it, you know, like where it could be. They even thought that it could have been taken to a country in Africa, whose people are black. There's a church there that they said housed the Ark. So, I wonder what is in that church, if the real one is in Israel now."

"I also heard this morning," I continued, "that they have taken the Ark to the new temple. They did it without announcing it so that there would not be any terrorist acts carried out. They had several Levi Priests there that carried it into the Holy of Holies. They said something about this being the Feast of Tabernacles and a holy day for Jews, which is why it was allowed in by God without anybody dying. *And* they are going to start back animal sacrifice!"

"Why, would they do that? I thought Jesus did away with that?" Anne looked puzzled.

"He did, but only the Christians believed it, not the Jews, you know they never accepted Christ as the Messiah."

Anne laughed, "Oh, I knew that, I just forgot we were talking about the Jews."

"Well, the same thing applies to Religious Groups, they only think of Jesus as a prophet and not the Son of God, whom they call Allah. Their prophet is Mohammad. The Jews are still looking for the Messiah, I don't know if the Religious Groups believed in a Messiah."

"There's a lot about the Jewish and Religious Groups' religions I do not know or how they foresee the future, but I am sure we will learn one day!" I concluded.

Chapter Eight

Each day there would be a small tidbit of news concerning both the Ark of the Covenant and Noah's Ark. It wouldn't be much but just enough to keep the story alive in the media.

Around the world there was an unusual calm, at the moment there were no major conflicts happening, which made us all relax and say 'we finally have world peace.' The Iraqi War was over, our servicemen were home with only the usual number stationed at bases around the world.

Although we still had the national terrorist alert system in place, it actually stayed in green most of the time. Since the death of Osama, we actually thought Al Qaeda had dispersed and was no longer a threat.

The threat of Iran some years back with the development of nuclear weapons was resolved and Iran allowed inspectors in to monitor their progress in acquiring nuclear power for peaceful use.

Then one evening during the news the Prime Minister of Israel had held a news conference which I happened to miss when it was covered live earlier in the day. It went like this, "Chancellor Jude the First has been in communication with the Jewish State of Israel. The talks between the Goveian and Israel have led to a trip for the Chancellor to visit the newly built temple in Jerusalem."

I paid no more attention to the story, like everybody else I had other things on my mind. Christmas was coming up and the Chancellor wanted to celebrate the Christmas Service in the Temple. Although Israel did not celebrate Christmas, they did celebrate Chanukah at about the same time. This gesture by Israel to the Goveian and the Chancellor was in hope of receiving more support from other world governments, which they hoped would establish their place permanently in the World.

Christmas morning rang in cold and clear in North Carolina, we no longer had visits from Santa Claus at our house, for Lexis was now fourteen and quite the teenager but we still opened our presents on Christmas morning.

However in other parts of the world, it was already Christmas afternoon or evening and as I prepared the turkey for the oven, I switched on the TV in the dining area of the kitchen. I flipped through the channels looking for one of my favorite Christmas movies, but halted on the Coxx Network when I recognized their breaking news' screen.

"Chancellor Jude has been here since early last evening and we will show you the Service that was conducted in the temple at daybreak in Israel."

As the correspondent described the scene in the large congregational area of the Temple, the camera spanned this great room. The Temple was packed with Christians and the Chancellor conducted the service in Latin. I found this boring and switched the channels again.

I found 'It's a Wonderful Life' on channel eleven, the ABC network, and listened more than watched it as I went about getting Christmas dinner together. I was expecting Art and family over in the afternoon to open gifts and Lance was going to pick up Bryce.

Suddenly I heard the tone on the television that always announced breaking news, it got my attention and I stepped around the table to get a better view of the set, an unrecognizable reporter was waiting for his cue to speak when the camera focused on him.

"We are sorry to interrupt your regular television viewing," he said. "But there are developments at the newly built Temple in Jerusalem. With special permission by the government and accompanied by two Levi Priests the Chancellor has entered what the Israelis call the Holy of Holies, which is where the Ark of the Covenant is kept. He was led in by the Priests, surrounded by four Deacons. Our television cameras are not permitted behind these curtains."

As the reporter spoke, we watched the small procession go behind the purple velvet curtains, and then the reporter spoke on for another two minutes or so as the camera stayed focused on the curtains. He was simply reminding us that this visitation was allowed because Israel wanted to cement their relations with Asbath, the Chancellor and the Goveian, in hopes that this would dispel threats coming from the Jehamic countries that surrounded the small nation.

Now they emerged from the Most Holy of Holies, and the Chancellor made his way back to the podium, again he made the sign of the cross and spoke in Latin, which a translator interpreted for us.

What it amounted to was the Chancellor wanted to set up a residence in Israel, so a small rendition of the Goveian was built inside the walls of the Temple. We also learned that this request had been granted by the Israeli government.

Second Event Chronicles

All seemed normal for the next few weeks, and although it was still winter, you couldn't tell it by the weather. It had been seven years since we had had more than a flake or two of snow.

I followed the progress of the Asbathian Principal Chancellor moving his home from Asbath to Israel. Construction was under way for the Chancellor's new residence in the holy city of Jerusalem. The new building was completed by mid-summer, and then in August, Chancellor Jude First moved in with great ceremony and with a speech.

What was said by the Chancellor sent shivers up my spine for it sounded as though he was claiming to be god on Earth.

"It is only right that God in the flesh have his headquarters in the holy city of Jerusalem. From here I can conduct the business of the Goveian as it was meant to be."

For some reason this did not set well with the surrounding Jehamic nations. Asbath sent forces into Israel to give protection to the Chancellor as he gradually took over the Temple. Israel was caught off-guard and did not know how to cope with this internal take over by the Goveian.

Then one morning in December, when I turned on the television for the morning news, I was presented with a picture of chaos! The scene being shown was that of military vehicles approaching Israel! It was unknown just to what country these weapons of war belonged, but Israel had already been struck with a nuclear bomb! A sneak attack and it was not known who launched the missiles! Initial reports were that a town in central Israel had been destroyed. It was Sunday morning here in the USA while in the Middle-East it was already mid-afternoon.

Everything was confusing and I had a hard time sorting out the information. I felt my heart pound as I knew in my mind that we were at war again and that this time nuclear weapons had already come into play.

Updates during the day were sporadic and non-conclusive, "The terrorist alert is set at red," reported ABC News.

"Forces being sent to Israel," reported CNN.

"As of this moment we still do not know who launched the missile," reported MSNBC.

The phone rang, it was Larraine, "Alice, I am terrified," she said. I could hear the anxiety in her voice. "I don't have anybody close by that I can really talk to, I miss my family."

I tried to present a calmness which I did not feel, "I know, I understand. I'm pretty shook up myself. The thing about all of this is, that there is no good information, no one knows what is going on or, if they do, they aren't saying."

"How could they not know who attacked Israel?" asked Larraine.

"Maybe they do and just aren't saying right now," I replied.

"God," Larraine was close to tears and I could tell she wasn't holding up too well, after a long pause she spoke again. "Lee and I've talked; we are coming back to North Carolina."

"When? How?" I asked for I knew how tight things were financially with them.

"We'll sell everything. We aren't bringing anything with us but our clothing. It'll take about a month, gosh. I hope we can hold out and I don't lose my mind."

"What about your animals?" I asked.

"It'll be hard, but I will try to find homes for them and if I can't, I'll..." here she stopped speaking and we both were silent, for I already knew what she would have to do.

"It'll work out. You got to have faith, we all do," I'm not too sure how convincing I was but I hoped that she believed me.

"I'm calling Clara tonight, she always said Lee and I could come and stay with her, I hope she hasn't changed her mind."

"I'm sure she will be tickled for you to live with her. She's been real lonely since Johnny moved out.."

We spoke on for a few more minutes, then said 'good bye' and hung up.

That night our female President called a news conference, all networks would carry it live and it was scheduled for eight o'clock. By the time it aired, I had talked with all my sisters on the phone and there were different speculations as to what was happening or what would happen.

After her introduction, she settled in at the podium and with a very grave expression, she began her speech.

"Good evening, I would first like to try and explained exactly what has occurred over the past thirty six hours or so.

Without warning or provocation, the small state of Israel has come under attack. For the first time since the bombings of Hiroshima and Nagasaki in World War Two, nuclear weapons have been used.

Deaths are estimated at three hundred thousand. This of course, will rise in number with the effects of radiation.

Israel's citizens have taken refuge in shelters, underground where possible. The government of Israel has declared war and we are having a difficult time holding them back from launching their weapons.

They have given the UN forty-eight hours before they act on their own.

I cannot emphasize strongly enough the world wide effect this will have. Recommendations will be issued for each local government as to what you as civilians should do to protect yourselves. I will not go over these at this time as it is more necessary at the moment to just fill you in on what is known.

It is still unknown what country sent this one missile, as it was launched by a submarine from the Indian Ocean. Intelligence suspects that somehow a nuclear sub has been hijacked by Jehamic extremists, thus knowing exactly who it is, will be hard to discover.

I have ordered troops into the Middle East and into Israel and at the moment there are five hundred thousand troops heading there.

Also for the first time since the late seventies, I am reinstating the draft. Any able-bodied man or woman eighteen to thirty five years of age will be contacted and reviewed for enlistment in the armed forces.

I have ordered our borders locked down, there will be no planes flying for the foreseeable future, only military and emergency aircraft will be permitted to fly.

We have declared military action on any extremist or terrorist organizations known or unknown."

Her speech continued for another thirty minutes but gave no more information than what she had already said.

We were at war again but against an unknown enemy. Sunday finally ended and Monday dawned dark and snowy. We hadn't had a good snowfall in quite some time, but warnings went out that it could be radioactive, highly improbable, but who wanted to chance it. Schools closed, and also many businesses, but people were afraid to venture out anyway.

Inside of our home we made an effort to plug up any opening that might allow in any contaminated air. I wouldn't allow my cats back outside and kept at least one TV turned to Coxx News.

Chapter Nine

The ink had barely dried on the pages of the newspapers the next morning when all hell broke loose in the *Yellow Stone National Park*. When I turned on the morning news the scene being shown was one of great billows of gray smoke covering the skies.

"What on Earth...." I spoke aloud.

I listened to the reporter, "... unexpected eruption occurred about eleven o'clock PM Mountain Time. Geologists have been monitoring the park for decades but even so this eruption was a surprise. We have no detailed information just now, as it is much too dangerous to approach the swelling mound that is forming, even as hot gases are escaping the newly born volcano."

To me it didn't look like it would be a great problem, for no lava was escaping, only hot gases. But as we watched during the day you could almost see a mountain growing, at which geologists weren't hiding their amazement and confusion. Not in recorded history and certainly not with people's ability to film and transmit pictures over the airwaves, has a volcano developed so quickly.

Meanwhile it was unbelievably cold, especially since our winters for the last several years had been so warm. Checking the thermostat showed a temperature of minus eighteen degrees, Fahrenheit! The windows had compilations of condensed water that of course had frozen and now was a thin layer of ice covering the inside of the windows!

All the heat we had was electrical and although the thermostat was set as high as possible, it was still freezing inside. Thomas had already lit the gas logs in the fireplace and that was the only place in the house where you could actually feel warmth.

Two days later, we learned that Israel, tired of waiting to find out who had launched the one nuclear missile, retaliated, and sent a barrage of regular warheads towards Iran! Well, at least they had not launched nukes, at least not yet. The Iranians were now dealing with the aftermath of about thirty Tomahawks, which dealt destruction onto the civilian population.

Their response was to declare a Jihad on the United States! They claimed that the USA had furnished Israel with the missiles, thus it was the United States that had attacked them.

In *Yellowstone National Park,* the mound had grown into a moderate mountain of about a thousand feet and still growing, with noxious gases continuously spewing from the crater at its center. Readings from seismographs were showing the possibility of an earthquake at any time but geologists were arguing among themselves as to where it would most likely occur. Even if they could agree it would make little difference, as there would be nothing that could be done.

Since the areas surrounding the park were sparsely populated, evacuations went fairly smoothly.

By the end of the week, our President had ordered all reserve units into active service as more troops were being transported to the Middle-East in response to both the nuclear attack on Israel and Israel's retaliation on Iran.

"Hello," I answered the phone; it was my oldest sister, Anne.

"Alice," she began. "Did you hear that there was another earthquake?"

"Where, at Yellowstone?"

"No, this one just happened in India!" said Anne. "I guess we were so busy watching Yellowstone that we weren't thinking it could happen somewhere else right now!"

"Let me get the news," I replied, as I carried the cordless into the living room and changed channels. I switched on Coxx News and immediately there were pictures from a helicopter high overhead showing demolished buildings and zoomed images of people panicking in the street.

"What have you heard," I asked.

"Nothing concrete," she replied. "You know what I think, Alice?"

"No, what do you have on your mind," I asked.

"I think we are in the beginning of the Great Tribulation."

I waited a moment for this idea to sink in before answering, "I hadn't really thought about that in a long time, I guess I had given up on it happening in my life time. If it is, all we can do is stick together and pray that we will be protected from what is about to happen!"

"Yeah, we can only guess. By the time we know for certain, it'll be over," she answered.

"Wow!" I said at the thought that Christ's return could be very close. There was a pregnant silence as we both became lost in our own thoughts.

After a bit, Anne broke the silence, "I wonder if anybody else has considered the possibility."

"Well, since the government banned the broadcast of religious programs, we really don't know what the different religions might think of this."

"I know, I still don't understand why congress passed that resolution," she replied.

"Well, they bowed to pressure by the atheists and other non-Christian groups, just like they were taking so many of the Christian symbols out of government places and schools; they finally took religion off the airways too. You know a lot of the denominations were destroyed by all the new laws and the few that remained have gone underground," I reminded her.

"I know, I can't even get my favorite Gospel music on the radio anymore. I have to play CDs if I want to listen to Gospel music."

"I know, it's been that way for a long while now. You know Larraine said she and Lee were heading home in about a month or so after they sell everything. She didn't say how they were coming, either by car or bus," I wondered.

"Too bad they stopped planes for everyday transportation; they could be here in a few hours. Well I gotta go; Wayne and I will drop by later this week, bye!"

"Okay, see you then, bye!" and I press the talk button on the phone to disconnect.

The next morning there was even more bad news on the airways, there was another major quake, this time off the coast of the Pacific northwest, the states of Washington, Oregon and the northern part of California!

During the night this new disaster had also produced a tsunami that even now was on its way across the Pacific Ocean heading for Japan, Taiwan and China. The Hawaiian Islands had already been completely wiped out by this huge wave, engulfing all the islands and they now lay under twenty or more feet of water!

Although Tsunami warnings had reached Hawaii in time for its citizens to head for high ground, this wave was reported to be over three hundred feet high, an astonishing height and, as the reporter said, unless they had reached the top of one of the many volcanoes on the islands, or the upper floors of some high-rise complexes, there would be few survivors.

As of this moment the estimate of the dead was in the hundreds of thousands for that tiny chain of islands. Scientists were stunned that a tsunami created so far north had reached the Islands; it had never been in any of the scenarios discussed over the decades.

The Pacific Coast of the US hadn't been spared either, for within minutes of the quake a hundred foot high wave took out all coastal towns and cities from Upper Canada to northern California. We were waiting for complete details but it seemed as though thousands had died and reports of billions of dollars in damage.

Later the next day, the volcano in Yellowstone National Park, finally erupted with a thunderous roar that I was watching at the time. Even the camera recording this event shook with the force of the eruption. As this was not an unexpected event, most of the networks were tuned into it when it happened.

"Oh my god," exclaimed the reporter who was on the scene but in a safe location. "From our station here in Jackson Hole, Wyoming, we can feel this building tremble and we are fifty miles away. We are transmitting pictures from the dirigible high over the park, as you can see there is now black smoke mushrooming from the volcano."

The reporter paused for a second as he touched his ear piece as though he was receiving new information, "I have just received information that the airship will be coming back to the station as it is getting unsafe for it to remain aloft. In case you are wondering, we were using a helium-filled dirigible because it was too dangerous for a helicopter to fly and now it looks like it is also too dangerous for the airship.

We will be switching to one of the cams that monitor the park from atop the Gallatin Mountain Range."

The scene now switched to a composite picture, four at a time on the screen, showing different angles of the same picture. I barely heard what the reporter was saying as I watched the screen. By now the volcano was visibly growing as if it was being blown up by an air pump. It grew and grew and all the while the smoke rose higher into the atmosphere and now the black smoke was reddish. I realized, as the reporter was talking, that lava had now reached the summit of the volcano and was being thrown out and up, along with ash, smoke and invisible gas!

I felt as though I was watching one of those disaster movies but with a twist, for my heart was pounding in my chest and my breathing very rapid. I knew I was having a panic attack and I felt as if I was dying. Lexis heard my call and came rushing into the living room.

"Grandma!" she cried when she looked at me. I caught a reflection of myself in the mirror over the mantel and saw just how white my skin was and knew I was close to fainting.

Lexis laid my chair back so that I was completely reclined and lying flat. She got me a glass of orange juice from the fridge and held it while I drank. I felt the blood come back into my head and the queasiness and lightheadedness began to disappear.

After a moment I was feeling better but I knew my near collapse was due to the fact that, yes, we were entering the Great Tribulation! From what I knew from having read the Bible and studies, that for the next three years or so, the Earth was in for a very difficult and destructive time and that many, many millions of people would die!

Somehow, I must deal with this and try to preserve my family for I knew few would believe me. I would just have to pray that my loved ones and I would be found worthy enough to come through these horrors, that man was bringing onto himself for all the years of disobedient and wanton sin against God and His Word.

North Carolina was still in the grip of a major cold spell, and now it had started raining! This didn't make any sense at all seeing how it was just above zero degrees here.

The weatherman explained it this way, "Yes, folks, it is raining and yet the temperature is nine degrees. The reason for this is the eruption of the volcano in Yellowstone National Park. With the large volume of ash suspended in the higher levels of the atmosphere, it is still very hot and thus warming the air and seeding the clouds. This causes unexpected moisture that is falling as rain instead of snow but it freezes on contact with the frozen surfaces, creating a very dangerous and potent ice storm.

"So be prepared for power outages and extremely bad driving conditions. If you haven't already done so, now is the time to get your generators running and to stock up on supplies for a long winter siege."

If that wasn't depressing enough, we were also dealing with an outbreak of the flu that no one was prepared for, so that this year's vaccinations were ineffective against it. As of this moment, no one in my household was sick. We had been housebound for some time now due to the dangerous cold. I had taken Lexis out of school, when I learned how cold the schoolrooms were. It wasn't too long afterwards, that they closed the schools for the Winter Break, they no longer called it *Christmas Holidays*.

Thomas took the grocery list I had written to the Food Lion down the road for the supplies we needed and to get kerosene for the generator we just recently purchased.

Art and Lance were both having difficult times trying to keep their homes and families together and I was halfway looking for either one or both to move back into my tiny two bedroom home. If they needed to, I couldn't tell them 'no', they were my sons and there was no way I could be happy if they weren't happy and safe.

Art and Kerry along with Brook and Art Jr. were finding it hard to keep their bills paid; Kerry's job with the cell phone company had taken a hit during the last economic set back and her hours had been cut in half and her health benefits discontinued. Now they were arguing over money, so what else was new, everybody was arguing over money.

Lance still wasn't married but had moved in with a girl a few years back, but they didn't have any children and so the only child Lance had was Bryce, with whom he received visitations every other weekend. He still worked as a mechanic but work was getting slack in that field too.

Things were tight all over; the price of oil was still fluctuating but the price never went lower than four dollars a gallon, but never more than the freeze of four seventy five that congress had mandated years before. So we had learned to cope and to budget our money to cover the necessities and do away with a few luxuries. I had kept my cable TV and internet connection though, for it was the only pleasure we allowed ourselves and the easiest way to stay connected with the rest of the world.

Chapter Ten

In the Middle East, the region was heating up rapidly and the Iranians had launched missiles back at Israel without so much as a complaint to the United Nations. These were not nukes, we learned later but biological warheads! We did not know yet what microbes had been released on the world but I was sure we would soon learn.

    As I kept track of the goings-on in the world, our situation here at home was not improving. The freezing rain had finally stopped but left a very thick coating of ice on everything. As foreseen, trees toppled from the weight of the ice and as they did, they brought down the power lines creating massive power outages across the state. But we were not alone, no, from the Atlantic to the Pacific, all were under this blanket of ice. Our neighbor to the north, Canada, was in much of the same shape as we. Plus this phenomenon was rapidly spreading south toward Mexico. It was just a matter of time before much of the world would be sharing our fate. The ash entering the atmosphere from the Yellowstone Volcano was still in enormous quantities so that, already, here in the States, we could scarcely tell night from day.

    Thomas managed to get the generator going and Lance asked if he and his girlfriend could come and stay here until things got better. I suggested that just he come and that his girlfriend go home to her parents.

I would not even listen to his argument and hung up the phone. Our space was limited and since she had somewhere she could go, it was best she did so. After all, I had nowhere they could sleep together and I would not have allowed it even if I had.

That evening Lance managed to get his old truck up the icy path to our house and he was alone. He entered carrying only one small duffel bag, he looked weary and hungry.

"Gosh, it's cold. I ain't never seen it this cold before. what the devil is going on?" he asked as he made his way to the living room where the gas fire was, the only heat we had. The generator kept the lights on but to run the heat pump would simply burn too much fuel, which was kerosene at three fifty a gallon.

Warming his hands by the fire he remarked, "At least y'all have this for heat. Janie and I didn't have anything after the electricity went. I don't see why she couldn't have come here too."

"We've been over this before," I told him. "You are not married and I might not be able to stop you from living together anywhere else but I can stop it here. Besides, we just don't have the room. You and your Daddy can set up the folding bed in the sunroom, but it will be mighty cold out there."

"I brought an electric blanket that was Janie's but she said she wouldn't need it at her folks. Where's Lexis?"

"She's in her room," I replied. "Lexis!" I called.

She came into the living room, a small girl for her age, but then she always had been, she was four foot ten inches tall and weighed ninety six pounds. Lexis had dark blond hair that she wore cut to just below the shoulders, and she had the largest, bluest eyes you could imagine. She was well mannered and a great deal of help to me around the house. I was now sixty five years old and although I had managed to drop fifty pounds, because of my bad knees, it was still painful doing many things. I think she was a Godsend to me at the time we adopted her.

"Yes, Grandma?" Then she saw Lance, "Uncle Lance," she squealed as he gave her a big hug. "Are you going to stay with us?" she asked.

"Yeah, 'till this freezing weather is gone, anyway."

"You can have my room," she offered.

Lexis had always been a very generous girl.

"Naw, I'll set up in the sun room, like before, remember?"

"Yeah. Where's Janie?" she asked next.

"She's staying with her folks for awhile," he informed her.

We got Lance settled and I began getting a meal together with Lexis' help.

"Grandma, the phone is for you," said Lexis handing me my cell phone. Since only a few people had my cell number and only called it when they couldn't get through on the regular phone lines, I became very concerned almost immediately.

"Hello."

"Hi Alice, it's me, Larraine," she said. "The ice storm has taken down many of the phone lines; I've been trying for hours to get through to any of you on the east coast. Anne's and Clara's cell phones aren't working; I was surprised that yours is."

"Yes, we are having sporadic phone service right now, which is why I am keeping the cell phone charged and turned on. How bad is it your way?"

"Well, not quite as bad here as where you are but we are expecting it to get worse over the next few days."

"Which is why I needed to call, it may be this summer before Lee and I can get out of Texas. With these icy conditions, it would be foolhardy to attempt a cross country drive right now."

"I agree with that, so.... What are you going to do?"

"The only thing we can do ... Wait until it gets better outside. At least Lee is still working some and it'll give me more time to find homes for my animals. That was worrying me ... a lot!"

I told Larraine to let me know if we could do anything here to help, which I knew there wasn't, she lived too far away.

"I will," she replied and we said 'goodbye.'

With the holidays over, we attempted to settle in and make the best of the situation, we couldn't change things, and so the only logical thing to do was be flexible and go with the flow.

Over the next six weeks or so, things were getting worse over there and the cold and icy weather kept the North American continent in an ice box. We did manage to get our electricity back on and you can believe me when I say, I will never take heat for granted again. I could finally get warm. But still the schools would not reopen until early May which meant the kids would have to make up this lost time in the summer.

Breaking news came to my ear and I quit what I was doing to listen better, the announcer was saying, "...arriving in the middle-east at about midnight our time last night. Israel has launched nuclear weapons toward Iran and now another nuke has struck Israel from the Indian Ocean. Ground combat is now out of the question. None of the Arab countries are allowing American troops to use their air bases. Europe has also closed their bases for use by the United States, only Britain is allowing us to land there.

Canada has offered to send more troops to the area but it is understood that they would prefer to stay as they are just now."

From what I could gain from the newscasts over the next few days, Europe was siding with the Arab nations! But why? Because of oil and the fear of not getting it! Old alliances were dying. Treaties were broken. No one was living up to their promises and the United Nations was bit by bit deteriorating, as one nation at a time pulled out and no longer wanted any part of it.

Asia, Japan and Taiwan, weren't much help to anyone or even themselves, for the Tsunami had destroyed so much of their homelands that it was all these nations could do to take care of their own, for there was no aid coming from the rest of the world, which were also dealing with major catastrophes.

The super volcano as the scientists called it, had the whole North American continent wrapped in a smoky blanket and now some of the ash was falling to the Earth. It made going outside near impossible. Surprisingly too, it was starting to warm up, which you would think was a good thing but scientists were now saying that we were heading for very hot weather, due to the ash holding in heat and carbon dioxide, creating a green house effect.

"Alice," it was Clara. "I think we need to go get Larraine and Lee!"

"I just talked with her a few days ago, Clara, and she said it would be a month or so. What has happened?"

"Lee has been laid off from his job and Larraine said that she has no more sewing customers. They aren't finding any buyers for their things and they can't make rent this month."

"Who do you think we can get to go? I think Art and Lance can if it's on the weekend. How about Rubin and Johnny?"

"Maybe so if it is on the weekend. But what will they drive?"

"Well Art has a mini-van, but I don't think all four are necessary, we'll ask all of them and see who it would inconvenience the least. Art's his own boss so I know he can work a schedule between jobs. Get back to me," and we said 'goodbye.'

We worked things out so that Art and Lance would take a long weekend to bring Larraine and Lee to North Carolina. The arrangements were made for two weeks, hopefully most of the ice would be gone and the ash in the stratosphere would hold off until they could get back.

Larraine said what they hadn't sold by that time, they were leaving. For weeks now since the eruption of Yellowstone's volcano, the entire country had been living under this thick shroud of volcanic ash, which for now was not falling to the Earth. This was both good and bad; if we ventured outside we wore gas masks to avoid inhaling what dust was in the air. Small amounts fell each day and it was a constant battle to keep roof tops and cars swept clean of the mess.

The weekend arrived for them to leave, we all chipped in for gas money and a U-Haul was rented to help bring back what they could of Larraine and Lee's personal belongings.

They left my house on a Friday morning at five, just before dawn. They had cell phones and chargers for those phones, food for a week and a couple changes of clothes. I watched from my kitchen window as they drove down my path to the main road and made a right turn towards 301.

Art called every couple of hours like I had asked him to, keeping us informed on where they were and what was happening. He told us that it was slow going due to the ash on the roads but that road sweepers and snowplows were being used by the Department of Transportation to help keep the roads as clear as possible. This was the case in every state they were in and if they were lucky they would stay behind a plow to enjoy relatively easy driving.

They left on a Friday morning and it should have taken them seventeen hours one way but it ended up taking a week to go and come back with Larraine and Lee! They came here first, to my house.

Larraine hugged me when she came in, "Boy, am I ever glad to be back in North Carolina. I hope to never leave it again."

Chapter Eleven

Clara came and got Larraine and Lee; Art and Lance took the few belongings they'd brought with them, which included two cats, to Clara's house. Travel was a little better toward Clara's residence as she lived further east towards the coast. The worst part of the ash cloud was over the central section of the United States.

We all breathed a sigh of relief that she and Lee had finally come back to North Carolina and that they were safe.

My brother Colin had also migrated north from Florida and settled in Greenville, North Carolina. My younger brother Drow dropped by fairly often now, whereas before we had gone fifteen years without seeing each other. The family was getting closer in miles and in contact. Only a few miles had separated some of us, yet I hadn't seen them since I had seen the ones living a thousand miles away.

Clara had guardianship of our youngest brother Carter and she was forced to bring him home to her house. He had stayed in an institution for much of his life but they no longer could care for their residents and were discharging the ones that had family with whom they could live.

Six months later, in November, we were still dealing with the fallout of the ash cloud but it was getting lighter. But it seemed that, as one catastrophe ended, another began. The War in the Middle East was little more than an attempt at total annihilation of Israel.

We only received sporadic video from that part of the world and anything 'live' was only occasionally transmitted. The United States was totally committed to the defense of Israel, we had sent hundreds of thousands of troops there for her defense, as had Britain and Canada.

The nations of Europe were forming a Joint Federation of Nations, a new government which was governed by the Chancellor, no less. What a shocker that was! He now ruled like an Emperor from the Temple in Jerusalem, having sided with the Arab nations in attempting to destroy Israel. As it turned out, the liaison that began in friendship had turned treacherous, for the Chancellor wanted to rule from the sacred temple in the Holy City of Jerusalem, as a god.

Many hundreds of thousands, if not millions were claiming divination of miracles by this Chancellor. Somehow, he had kept the city of Jerusalem intact although there was devastation surrounding the great city. It was as though the city was shrouded with divine protection, where not even nuclear weapons came anywhere near.

The United States had managed to evacuate the small country, as many Israelis, with only what they could carry, were boarded upon huge helicopters and flown out to waiting battleships, aircraft carriers and cruise liners. They had made the six week long trek across the Atlantic, where they were dispersed and taken to special hotels, and military bases to be assimilated into the United States. The State of Israel was no more.

All that remained untouched was the City of Jerusalem and the Holy Temple where the Chancellor resided.

Although it might seem improbable, we were still receiving news by way of television and we always had some sort of power, be it from the power companies or from our generator. The cable companies were hard put to, to stay on the air, so much of our information was received through the antennas of our battery operated television. It was like someone wanted the world to see and hear what was happening in the Holy Land.

"These two men seem to have materialized from nowhere. No one knows precisely who they are, but they are at the gates of the temple demanding that the Chancellor leave this Holy Shrine. They are denouncing him as an enemy occupier of the Holy City of Jerusalem."
The pictures we saw were of two men that were dressed in fawn-colored robes, with large hoods that covered their features; they held an oil lamp in one hand and a shepherd staff in the other. They looked for all the world like Biblical prophets of old.
Their faces were in shadow and the sleeves of their robes covered their hands so you could not tell their race or nationality. They wore heavy chains for belts and an occasional peek revealed that they wore scandals. The robes were clean although they looked as if they were very old, tattered and made of burlap.

This wasn't recent news. It had been reported more than a year ago right after the bombing of Israel but at first no one knew what to make of it and only checked in on the strangers whenever other news waned.

Second Event Chronicles

Now, as the New Year approached, the past few years' events were being rehashed and this was a recording of the first encounter with the two. They had set up a tent just outside the walls of the temple and each day they walked in a small circle with one circling clockwise and the other counterclockwise and when they met each other they bowed low and continued their journey. The entire time they could be heard uttering a prayer-like chant, which no one could understand.

The few times that a reporter had spoken with them, they spoke in what I heard as English, yet the rest of the world heard in their native languages. Yet no one seemed to know it at the time. We all thought that they spoke our language and used an interpreter for others. It was months before this was realized. Protestant Christian clergymen declared this a miracle and deemed them prophets.

The prophets denounced the Chancellor, accused him of occupation of the Holy Temple, and demanded he leave.

They gave the Chancellor a new title, 'the False Prophet', and when asked what that meant they would not reply but continued their trek and their chant.

Once the prophets were approached by the Chancellor's guards, a small group of about a dozen men. There were harsh exchanges, when the soldiers attempted to remove the two, large fireballs fell from the sky and set fire to the soldiers' uniforms, and they fled the scene.

At one point, the two had knelt in the sand, facing each other, bowed low over their folded hands and touched their heads to the ground and when the prayer was done, they rose and raised their staffs into the air and vocalized loudly. Nothing was noted at the time, but within a few weeks, reports began of the rains having failed in many parts of the world and in others unusually heavy rains resulting in floods. Some areas were spared, yet no one related this to the prophets, at least not at first, not until they proclaimed it so and demanded that the Chancellor leave the Temple and the world would be restored.

Inland lakes, rivers, and seas turned a rust red color and all over the world, fish died and floated to the surface or were washed up on the water's edge where they rotted and defiled the air with their stench.

This was an event known as the Red Tide, an overgrowth of red algae that bloomed every few years. Yet this time it was worldwide, and decent drinking water became almost non-existent. If you were lucky, you had a well and just might have fresh water to drink. We were lucky; we did have a well and had never paid the three thousand dollars to hook up to the city water lines, which received their drinking water from the Tar River. This was now polluted with the red algae and was unfit to drink; the water treatment plants could not remove all of the impurities and people were instructed to boil it before drinking. Boiling it may have destroyed the bacteria but the horrible odor remained.

Several more attempts were made to remove the prophets by Asbath, yet they defied armies and still they prophesied.

Chapter Twelve

Meanwhile, the small nation of Israel was no more, all that remained was the land that it once occupied, and that laid in ruins. The Chancellor began in earnest to restore the land and renamed it, 'New Goveian City,' removing that status from Asbath to Jerusalem.

For what seemed like an unlikely union, the Goveian and the Jehamic nations and much of Europe was now under the rulership of the Chancellor, and he demanded complete and total loyalty and in a way, worship. He was, he declared, the embodiment of God on Earth and he would bring peace and prosperity to the world and the world fell for his charismatic and authoritative persona.

These nations which formed an alliance with the Goveian did so for their own survival, for the oil producing countries were part of this Joint Federation and members were given priority over any other nation. This left the United States, Canada, Britain, Japan, China and Australia as a non-declared coalition and, as such, they began to talk. These talks led to an unforeseeable declaration of war! Yes, there was no other possibility for they were starved of energy. The prices being demanded by, no longer OPEC, but a new alliance dubbed United Veneration of the Eastern Hemisphere, or UVEH, were too high and could not be met without serious consequences to the economy of these nations. Oftentimes they flat out refused to sell to the 'Great Satan.'

So when demands for crude were denied, these countries met in an undisclosed locale, but thought to be in Australia's noted outback bush country, in a secluded privately owned ranch, for this summit. When they emerged back in the United States, the leaders appeared together on television and the announcement was made - War, if UVEH did not agree to ship oil and to lower prices, and they were only given two hours to accept or face dire consequences.

All this time troops were amassing in a valley just outside of Jerusalem, a buildup by the Joint Federations of Nations in anticipation of something, what, the world did not yet know. (But we all had an opinion on it.)

"Alice, are you home?" it was Anne at my back door. It was a Sunday afternoon in October, and we were having a gathering of the sisters and brothers.

"Yes, come on in," I called back as I left the television in the living room to greet her and Wayne. "I was watching the news," I said as we entered the kitchen at about the same time. "Y'all the first ones here, the rest should arrive within the hour. Have you heard what our President and the Coalition have just announced?"

"No, we've been out this morning and haven't been back to the house, what's going on?" Anne asks as we all headed into the living room.

"They have in effect declared war on the JFN if they do not lower prices on oil and agree to ship ten million gallons to us, and they have only two hours to give an answer."

"Damn," declared Anne, "That went into the works rather quickly didn't it? What do you suppose their answer will be?"

"Your guess is as good as mine," I responded. "The United States can't declare war without congress voting on it and that could take several weeks or maybe even a month or so."

Later, after everybody had arrived at my house and we were enjoying a pot roast and talking about what the JFN would do, the quietness was suddenly interrupted by a loud whine and whishing noise that went over head. We stared at each other.

"What the hell..." shouted Colin. "That sounds like a squadron of jets."

Sure enough, as we all ran to the windows to get a glimpse of this obvious picture of impending war, we could see the sky dark with hundreds of warplanes, black stealth bombers, all in formation heading east, out toward the ocean. Then a much louder roar and the recognizable chop of helicopters following behind the jets, only they took a more northern turn.

"My God," squealed Clara. "What's happening?"

"We're at war!" Colin responded.

"I would say so," Thomas agreed as he stood behind me with his hands on my shoulders, which for some odd reason reminded me of the first time I had met him, when he did the same thing, as he declared, 'Look Boyce, she's cute.' What an odd time for that memory.

We were now married for forty eight years and had been through a lot and now we were going through something much worse than anything we had ever experienced before, not even the death of our son Thomas Jr. would prove to be as devastating as what we were about to face now.

Then from the television in the living room came the unmistakable tone, a very loud pulsating low pitch tone, which was use for emergency conditions. At once we turned our attention to it.

"This is an alert from the national defense agency. This is not a drill!! Take immediate action. Take shelter in basements or other inner rooms. Missiles are heading across the Atlantic, intended for various targets across the nation. Take shelter immediately!"

The siren kept sounding and the announcement repeated as a crawl bar instructed us to tune to channel thirteen for further information, which we did.

This was coming from an unknown location and an unfamiliar announcer, a short, stout, balding black man of about sixty or so and he had a small stack of papers in his hand that he was getting ready to read when we tuned in.

"Sorry, for the interruption of your Sunday afternoon, but as of two fifteen, just twenty minutes or so ago, our ultimatum was answered by an unannounced attack, as missiles of unknown origin are at this moment streaking across the Atlantic, heading for large metropolitan areas of the United States and Canada. Washington DC, New York, and bases in Cherry Point, North Carolina and ..." Here he named several more cities across the eastern seaboard, whose names ran together as one, as shock set in that missiles were heading for North Carolina.

For what seemed like hours, no one spoke; we just stood there and stared at the television as though it was the only link we had with the outside world, and it was.

"Please remain in your homes; do not go into the streets. An immediate curfew is in effect. All vehicles on the roads will be stopped and checked and taken into custody for the duration."

"'Duration of what?" I asked.

"He's not saying," replied Clara. "Alice, it looks like you have us all for houseguests for awhile. There's no way for me to get back to Williamston or any of you to get home for that matter."

So, we sat down and waited. For what? It was soon answered as we could hear the distant sound of explosions, missiles hitting their targets or else being taken out by counter forces. I had all of my siblings with me. Art and Lance with Kerry and the kids and Bryce were at Lance's house just across the way and it would seem we would all stay where we were for the time being.

Each of us told where we thought our children were at that moment and phone calls were made to try and find out just where everyone was and to let each other know if we were in safe places for now.

So far so good. We decided that we needed to ask for divine intervention and for protection. I led us all in prayer. Why I was asked to do so is beyond me, no more than we were in my home at the time and Thomas as head of household, never did any praying out loud.

We bowed our heads, and held hands, and I prayed, "Most gracious and loving heavenly Father. We know that our needs are already known by you so I will only ask that you remember us and place your protection upon us and our love ones. As we are sinners we recognize the need to be forgiven and at this time we ask that we are. May this world see the truth and recognize the need to return to Your worship. I pray in the name of Your one and only Son, Jesus Christ, our Lord and Savior. Amen."

"Amen!" everyone responded.

Sleeping arrangements were as such, Lexis would join me and Thomas in our bed, Anne, Larraine, and Clara would take Lexis' bed, the rest would sleep one on the sofa, in the three lounge chairs which laid out flat, and one on the sectional hide-a-bed which was only a twin-sized.

Thomas, and the other grown men walked over to Lance's house to make sure they understood what was going on, then we all settled in for a long wait.

Chapter Thirteen

Over the next few hours, overnight and on into the next day, air battles raged in the distance. The initial missiles were followed about two hours later by more of the same. Bombs fell all around us as we watched the night time sky light up like the Fourth of July.

The tenseness of it all had us screaming each time we heard the whistle of missiles streaking overhead, certain that this time we would be hit, but luck stayed with us and we were spared a direct hit.

Tuesday dawned with the smell of smoke and a dense fog which was smoke from distant fires. None of us had slept the previous two nights and our nerves were frayed but for the moment all outside was silent. We still had electricity which in itself seemed like a miracle, and all through the last two days the local emergency station had stayed on the air. We learned that the broadcast was coming from our own local television station, WHIG. The networks had gone off the air and there was no cable, so it was only through rabbit's ears that we were able to receive any kind of information.

"I really need to get home," said Clara. "I need to check on my kids. Sometimes, I worry too much about them."

"I know, we all are worried, maybe something can be straightened out today and everyone can go home."

It was hard to pretend that things were normal, although there was no damage in my yard, the smoke, thick overhead, told a different story of damage elsewhere. The sisters sat around my kitchen table drinking our morning cup of coffee while everyone else found where they could, to accommodate their attempts at eating or drinking. We were packed in my small house like sardines.

"I wish I knew why we were attacked," said Clara.

"They don't need a reason," replied Larraine with a bit of cynicism to her voice and I think we all understood what she was implying. "It should be plain to all of you by now that the United State is hated worldwide and has been for a good many decades now, if not a century or two.

"They want our money in charity and our soldiers for their defense, yet would stab us in the back and not think twice about it at the first opportunity. They say they don't want the United States policing the world but yet we are who they turn to, when they are in trouble."

"Not anymore, hadn't you noticed?" I interrupted her. "They now turn to the Chancellor in Jerusalem and so far he has come through. See how he has united all of Europe under one flag, now called the Joint Federation of Nations? They don't need the United States anymore and they want to get rid of us and the best way to do that is to starve us of energy. Many people are blind and don't see that, not even our government. It is time this nation woke up to what the rest of the globe thinks of us. Get out of their countries and let them go to rot for all I care. I for one am tired of all of it. Aren't y'all?"

Everybody nodded their heads.

"I've been tired of it," I said. "When I was online so much at one time, when I had the web-site, remember?

Second Event Chronicles

You couldn't find anybody on the web from other countries that wasn't bad-mouthing the United States. I mean, it even came from our own countrymen. I almost thought they wanted this country to be taken over or something and, you know what, it almost has been."

"If only we weren't so dependent on foreign oil," said Anne.

"We aren't or don't have to be," said Colin coming in on the conversation, while pouring himself another cup of coffee then walking over to the table where we were. "If it weren't for the environmentalists in this country the United States could provide four fifths of our own needs for fossil fuel. Plus it would keep many good paying jobs located here at home, rather than outsourcing so many of them overseas."

"At one time," Colin continued, "we were trying to develop new varieties of fuel and hybrid cars, it looked like things were moving along pretty steady then suddenly development stopped and we became even more dependent on foreign oil. You know what happened, don't you?" he added.

"The big oil countries put a stop to it, I bet," I said.

"That's it," Colin agreed.

"Why would they do that?" asked Clara.

Colin held out his right hand and rubbed two fingers together and answered, "Money! What else?"

Clara shrugged her shoulders as if that didn't make a bit of sense and Larraine enlightened her with, "Everybody isn't as honest as you are Clara."

"Besides all of this," I added as I waved my hand through the air, "There's something more important happening here that no one has mentioned yet."

With all eyes focused on me, now Drow entered in on the conversation, when he had previously just stood in the doorway listening. He piped in with, "You're not going to tell us it's the end of the world, are you?"

"As we know it, it is," I said bluntly. "I know many of you know your Bible, can't you see the signs?"

"This mess's been going on for almost fifteen years, now," argued Drow. "I don't believe all that hogwash anymore. I listened to the preachers preach all my life saying Jesus Christ is returning soon. Shoot, nobody knows that, the Bible tells us that. If you want my opinion on this mess, there's no heaven, no hell, no God and no Devil. When we die, we die! That's it. *The end!*"

There was a stunned silence in my small kitchen as everyone took in the shock of what he had said. The silence didn't last long however, the room lit up as simultaneously lightning flashed and thunder rumbled, making everyone jump and the women scream.

The thunder rolled for several minutes with a deafening roar that would not end but at last it did, and we all turned accusing eyes on Drow who had the sense to look embarrassed.

"Why is everybody looking at me?" he stammered.

"You don't know?" asked Larraine, as she cocked one eyebrow that made me think of Daddy. "Ever heard of God striking non-believers? Well, I think he was aiming at you."

At that we all laughed softly but each wondered if maybe...

As we were all lost in our thoughts, pondering our own self doubts and convictions, the announcer on the radio intruded and we turned our attention to it.

"...lifting the curfew of the last few days, citizens have the daylight hours to..."

So, everyone acted quickly, wanting to get to their own homes to be with their children and grandchildren. Stores were opening to allow the populace to stock up on goods and this must be done before nightfall when the curfew would once again be employed.

We learned over the next few hours that the Chancellor was demanding that if the Coalition wanted oil their citizens must swear an allegiance to the Goveian and to prove this allegiance, the head of each household would be issued a special number in order to buy fuel. And believe it or not, our government was considering it. Maybe as a nation we had no choice but as individuals, we did.

A month after the missiles fell on American soil; we once again were receiving shipments of oil from the Far East. Tankers were heading across the Atlantic right now and official government letters were reaching the homes across the nation.

We received ours on a Wednesday, delivered by special post requiring a signature at its reception. The letter was addressed to head of household, Thomas T. Nickolas. It was a form document, with a typewriter filling in the blanks. A form must be signed by both husband and wife and returned, and then a card would be issued with our number, granting permission to purchase oil products, from gasoline to kerosene. We signed and I mailed it back, by registered mail. About a month later our cards came in by registered mail. It was much like the card we used a few years ago to buy gas when it was rationed, and used the same way. Only this card had a picture of the newly built temple and a likeness of the Chancellor pictured in front of it, on the face of the card.

So, things were looking up, once more we could buy reasonably priced gas.

Chapter Fourteen

Now we could breathe a sigh of relief, I remembered thinking. It never occurred to me that our country would not be better off signing this pact with the Goveian, but that is exactly how it turned out!

This card, when I looked at it was shocking, when I read the numbers. Remember how credit cards' numbers of the different companies were all the same for that company, except for the last few digits that identified the card as yours and yours alone? Well, this card number read like this, 666-Asbath-and then your number like 123-A; well, 666-Asbath-130-C was our card number!

I had a very bad feeling about actually using this card for my instinct told me that this was the sign of the beast and by using it we would lose any spiritual protection we had thus far enjoyed. I refused to allow Thomas to use it; I took both cards and hid them until I could talk with my siblings and gain their opinions on the use of the card.

I called Anne first for I knew she was a bit more spiritually-minded than the others and had deep thoughts on such things.

"Hi," I began, and, after our informal greetings to each other I got around to why I had called her. "Have you received your card for buying gas in the mail yet?"

"Yeah, just this morning, why?"

"What do you think about the numbers?" I questioned with a bit of uneasiness in my stomach.

"I haven't looked at the cards real good yet, you sound funny, is something wrong?"

"I think so, get your cards and read the numbers to me," I instructed.

"Hold on," and she left and quickly returned, "Let's see, my card reads 666-Asbath-490-M, oh my God," she exclaimed. "Oh my God!"

"Is that what I think it is?" I asked.

"It doesn't look good," Anne replied. "It's got to mean what we think it does and Alice, if we use these cards I believe we will be swearing allegiance to the beast! Now, I know we are in the end time."

"If we don't use them, we can't buy gas and how then would we get around?" I asked in a high pitched voice which revealed the apprehensiveness I was feeling.

"Horse and cart," she replied.

"Horse and cart? Anne, have you lost your mind?" I thought maybe she had.

"Remember Jem, she and John have a horse ranch, we can buy horses from them."

"By golly, I think you are on to something. Call her and then get back to me," and we hung up.

A month or so later, all of my brothers and sisters had purchased a couple of horses and buggies. We did as the Amish did, and it wasn't as hard to do as you might think, not for us, but a little more so for our children and grandchildren. You see, as children born in the 1940's and early fifties, we had been around this mode of transportation before and we still had the ability to hookup and guide the animals and to care for them.

Of course Anne's daughter, Jem and her husband John were valuable in the knowledge that they had and they taught the rest of the grown children and grandchildren. We destroyed our gas cards and parked the vehicles one by one as they gave out of gas, relics of another era!

But a good many of our neighbors and friends thought we were insane! No wonder, for many did not see this as we did and who's to say we were right? We were following our own instincts for survival, not just physically but spiritually as well!

We did run into problems with local governments with their zoning laws and where farm animals could be housed, so to solve that dilemma, we leased pasture land not too far from us. Nowhere in the code though did it say we couldn't use them for transportation if our religious beliefs commanded it and they did!

Electricity for home use was no major problem because with the shortage of oil to burn to create electricity, our state and most of the rest of the country had built nuclear power plants. It was a necessary evil in this new environment we now found ourselves.

Once again we settled into an informal routine. Then over the airways came distressing news, there was another major confrontation with the two unknown prophets camped out at the gate of the Goveian City II complex in Jerusalem.

I watched in dismay as these two men were gunned down where they had lived for a year or more, in an ambush carried out by the Goveian's guards. There they lay, in a crumpled bloody mass with the Chancellor refusing to permit their bodies to be removed, stating that they were an example of what would happen, if or when someone else stood in opposition of God's Holy City and his delegate here on Earth.

Just after this incident there was a major gathering of armies by the Chancellor, in a valley just south of Jerusalem, claiming they were to defend the city from anyone wanting to revenge the deaths of the two transgressors, as he called them.

For over three days the cameras remained focused on their bodies lying so still where they had fallen and the news channels kept a small window open at all times with a view of the massacre, as if waiting. Waiting for what? To see if someone would try and remove the bodies? Or just perhaps watching them as they decayed into nothingness? That was anybody's guess. In any case, it really was a major distraction, as well as a disturbing one, to have at all times, as you would try to hear and watch the world news.

Then over the regular airways came a breaking news announcement, "Good evening, there are reports of an unusual occurrence at the locale where the two victims were assassinated a few days ago. It looks as if the bodies are stirring. Speculations are that this is a natural phenomenon of settling of the bodies as the flesh dissolves. In the unusual atmosphere of a hot arid desert, decomposition can proceed quite rapidly!"

As we listened to the reporter, the cameras were aimed at the two corpses, as they had been now for days, and like watching a movie about zombies, these two corpses slowly rose to their feet! Their robes fell away from their mangled bodies as they stood, revealing bloody and mangled flesh that began falling off of the bones. But the two disgusting figures began their march in clockwise and counter clockwise circles, leaving bits of rotting flesh as they marched!

However as we watched, the bodies began to flesh out with luminous muscle and then skin! Now totally nude, they continued their trek in new bodies that shimmered. The hair re-grew on their bald skulls, and this hair looked like spun silver!

Now, the two picked up their filthy, torn and bloody robes and put them on. Doing so transformed the robes and they became as white as freshly fallen snow and looked to be made from the finest silk with gold sashes about the waist. They retrieved their staffs which were now rods made of gold instead of wood.

Then quite suddenly, as if watching them come back to life was not miraculous enough, the two seemed to know that the world was watching through a camera. That was so far away to be certain that it was unseen by them, yet they faced in that direction.

"Citizens of the world," they spoke! Yes, once again their message was going out to all the Earth in languages that everyone could understand.

"We are witnesses to the one true and only God, Yahweh. Glory to His most holy Name and glory to the Son, Yeshua, the Christ. We bear truth and identify the Dragon, Satan, Lucifer! His time is ending!"

As they were speaking a fine silver mist began surrounding them and formed like a cloud at their feet. Now they were rising, ever so slowly into the sky. They began singing a song but no one could understand the words. In about fifteen minutes they were high in the sky but very visible from the camera lens, and suddenly they disappeared! They vanished, they had entered another realm, they did not leave the Earth, only its visible spectrum.

All this time, the announcer was silent, as though words were not needed, or perhaps he could not describe what we all were seeing. But, now he found his voice.

"Folks, I think that we have just witnessed a miracle! There can be no other explanation for what we have just seen! The two men had been pronounced dead by the Goveian physician. I do not know what we can expect from the Chancellor now."

The reporter continued on and then replays of the resurrection and ascension began to dominate the news for the next few weeks!

Chapter Fifteen

"And more religious fanatics have been rounded up," reported the commentator. This was not breaking news but just part of an interesting series of events that was thought not to have any real significance in world affairs.

This had been going on in abundance for the last few months now, whereas before only occasionally were fanatics taken very seriously. After the appearance of the two prophets at the gate of the temple wall, who had declared the Chancellor to be the false prophet or anti-Christ, many sects that were little known to most of the world had sided with these two and began making their existence known by demonstrating against the Asbathian Principal Church!

With this encouragement, their message was growing in scope and scale, and the authorities thought that it might create worldwide rebellion among the populace and quietly began to take action against them.

"Secretly, the army working under orders of the Goveian in Asbath, have been actively seeking out any non-Christian sect and arresting them in Europe and North Africa. According to our undercover journalists this is just now coming to light. They risked their lives to smuggle out these pictures that you are about to see. Be warned, they are graphic and you might want to remove small children and sensitive individuals from the room while they are aired."

What we saw as the commentator continued with his narrative were small Protestant churches, where the ministers and their congregation were unceremoniously dragged outside, bound, then loaded into buses and driven away; then the churches were set afire.

Yes, some of the pictures shown were difficult to watch, for the least bit of resistance often received very harsh treatment, from brutal beatings to outright death, either by a gun or a bayonet. Although the most graphic screens were edited, the bodies could be seen twitching and bleeding as the executioners laughed with no sympathy and left them to die where they fell.

Later pictures showed ravens and vultures and wild animals feasting on the remains of the dead. Their bones remained there until bleached white by the sun, with no Christian burial allowed for them.

These churches were of mixed races and various denominations of the Protestant religion, which had always been a thorn in the side of the Asbathian Principal Church since its founding some seventeen hundred years ago.

You would think that the Jehamic community would have been the biggest threat to the Christians, since the crusades were directly fought against them hundreds of years before, but no, it was this small Sabbath keeping group that irked the Goveian more than the Religious Groups; and now that the two had formed an alliance it would seem that they were of like-mind.

Now the scene returned to the field reporter, "This activity has the sanction of the Asbathian Principal Church and is not considered illegal. Trials are conducted and the members are given a chance to reject their beliefs and swear allegiance to the Church, or are harshly penalized. It is sad to report that not many are rejecting their beliefs and are being sentenced to prison time and the elders of these churches are often sentenced to death, especially those who openly condemn the Chancellor as being "the abomination of desolation that stand in the most holy place" is how they voice it, which is a quote from Matthew 24:15."

For the first time, it occurred to me, that this could be the slaughter of the Saints, but I had no way of knowing. Although I considered myself a Christian, I must admit that I did not attend church on a regular basis and was not a member of any denomination. I didn't feel guilty about this, maybe I should, but it was just that the churches around me all gave different interpretations of scripture and I was uncertain which was truthful, so I stayed away.

But I thought to myself, that at least this could not happen here in the United States, boy was I mistaken, howbeit on a smaller and not so deadly a scale.

Some years before, when the ACLU were actively campaigning to remove any religious symbols from our schools and government buildings and/or property, any kind of prayer or oath taken on the Bible or any religious type book, like the Quran and the Torah had been ordered illegal. Constitutional amendments had been added, making any contact between any religion and the US government, from local to national, unlawful. We had been living with that for some time now. All religious programming was taken off of the airways, be it television or radio. It was forbidden for people to go door-to-door promoting any religion. Prayer in public was forbidden, although a person could have a moment of silence if they wished to pray in public.

Some weeks later, with me following any news' reports on the destruction of churches in Europe and Africa, there came a small summit between the few remaining world leaders. Our President was compelled to attend. Since the United Nations disbandment about eighteen months ago, no such gatherings of Heads of State had taken place.

This summit happened of course in Israel, in Jerusalem at the Temple itself.

"We are forbidden to film inside of the temple," the reporter was saying, "so we only have the transcripts of the day's events to report.

The Chancellor himself has requested that all nations actively remove and arrest any opposition to the Church or risk losing their oil vouchers.

The United States has refused, stating the separation of any religion and the government ties their hands - as long as the religions stay out of the public limelight and do not actively campaign on the airways or public or government property, they are lawful.

What the religious leaders do in their churches and on private property, as long as illegal activities are not conducted, is no business of the government."

Well, the United States was not bowing to the veiled threats of the Joint Federation of Nations; this gave me back a sense of national pride. We needed to retain our strong appearance to the rest of the world.

When the United States took this stance, she was followed by her fellow coalition countries, Canada, Great Britain, Japan, China and Australia! Who would have thought that they would follow suit! This seemed to outrage the Chancellor for he was reported to have turned bright red in the face. Some swore you could see steam rising from his collar, their imagination I am sure, but still an interesting observance by those who professed to have seen it, swearing it to be so.

Of course the vouchers for all countries of the coalition were revoked and now we were back at square one. There were always those who would disagree with their Head of State and openly rebel and demonstrate against government policy, and so this began a new round of demonstrations in all countries. This was a vicious circle and I for one was becoming quite dizzy from it.

But in the United States, the government stood firm and sent the National Guard to deal with any of these mobs that attempted to attack the churches and do as the Chancellor had requested. A few clergymen and parishioners were injured, but none killed outright, before the members of these mobs were taken into custody.

However, the oil no longer flowed and once again the citizens were being rationed; this did not upset my family for we had already switched to other means of transportation and soon found our neighbors doing likewise.

As a result, the Goveian ordered a troop build-up in the Megiddo Valley, just south of Jerusalem. This was a well-known battlefield, which dated back through biblical times until today, where many famous battles had been fought.

Why did the Chancellor choose such a well-known place for his armies? The United States took this as a challenge and began a call up of men for enlistment or reinstatement into the armed forces.

The ringing of the phone startled me out of a late afternoon nap, I moaned as I reached for the receiver, "Hello."

It was Anne, "Alice, Jake has been drafted."

I sat up, wide awake, "I thought he was exempt, whatever happened?"

"We thought so too, after all he is in his first year of college and he is just nineteen. Wendy just called me; she was crying her heart out."

"Isn't there anything she can do?" I asked.

"They are looking into it, but I don't think there is much that can be done."

"He can enlist," I said.

"Why do that?" she replied. "They've been doing all that they could to keep him out."

"Well, if he goes ahead and enlists, now that he knows his number has been called, he can at least choose what branch of the service he wishes to enter. Plus, if he chooses the National Guard or the Coast Guard, at least he would stay state-side," I explained. "Isn't that better than being sent to the middle-east right now? That's where the military will be going, I understand. Something about taking over Iraq, I guess the way we invaded back in two thousand and three, only this time we are going for the oil. I guess we have no choice; after all they have called our country out this time, that's how I see it. They know that we must have energy and if they are going to keep dangling it over our heads like a mouse to a cat, then sooner or later the cat is going to jump and I think we are jumping!"

And jump we did, not only us but the coalition too, within eight weeks we had new troops heading over there along with the other nations of the coalition. The trip took about six weeks; all armies from every corner of the world were heading for the Valley of Megiddo.

As the battleships carrying troops headed in that direction our scientists had another concern. An approaching comet had suddenly appeared in the night time sky.

Chapter Sixteen

There was an informal and unplanned gathering at my house, it just seemed to happen with all my siblings calling within an hour of each other, wanting to know if I would be home or did I have anything planned. To each my reply was the same and to say that so and so had just called asking the same question and they were on their way over at that very moment.

"Alice, I'm coming in," Clara arrived first, which was unusual for she is no early bird and often the last one to get anywhere.

"C'mon in," I called back. "I feel honored," I laughed, "everybody is coming here today and it isn't even a special occasion and it is raining and cold!"

"This war has me frozen with fear," confided Clara, "and now, what is this thing in space that has the scientists all worked up!"

Soon, all of my brothers, Carter with Clara, my sisters and a few nieces and nephews, as well as my two sons had managed to crowd into my small home. Everybody was talking at once and we sounded like a congressional meeting in progress at the Capital.

"The Megiddo Valley where all these armies are gathering is the place where the battle of Armageddon will be fought," said Colin beginning the topic that was on everyone's mind.

"But, isn't the Battle of Armageddon supposed to be a worldwide battle?" I asked. "All the nations of the Earth are supposed to do battle with each other and be spread across the globe with no nation being spared. If all the armies are heading for the Middle-East, perhaps we will not have war on American soil, at least that's what I'm hoping for!"

"Many possibilities exist," declared Anne, "and I don't think we are supposed to know for sure exactly what will happen or where it will happen."

"You understand," chimed in Clara, "that Revelations or John said what would happen if certain things were not corrected. So, as a nation, if we turn to God and pray for forgiveness, then as a nation, we should be spared."

"How can that be done," I asked, "when all religious programming and spreading the word of God from door to door has been banned?"

"I admit that I don't have the answer for that," Clara replied. "I'm not one for breaking the law. It carries a heavy penalty, like a five thousand dollar fine or five years in prison, or both!

"I know, I shouldn't be telling this but my church holds a bingo game night and invitations are placed in the newspaper inviting people to come and play. After they arrive they are given their game cards with Bible verses printed at the bottom of each page. No law is broken because it is done on church property and if anyone does not want the card with the verses on them, then they must leave because all cards have them. A short sermon is given along with an invitation to repent and accept Christ and a prayer. We even might sing a hymn. You will be surprised at how many are thankful for this and many admit to missing religion on TV and radio."

"Back to the 'all nations' statement, if you think about it, all the nations are being represented there," said Colin raising one brow as he glanced to each of us.

"We really do not know what God's plan is, do we?" I added. "After all His Word does say 'if mankind repents and turns back to God' then what has been predicted would be changed, right?"

"That's how it appears to me," said Larraine speaking at last. She had been unusually silent for a while as she always thinks things through before making a statement. Lee stood behind her chair and kind of nodded as though agreeing with her.

"I've been following the path of this comet," said Lee. "Have any of you?"

Some nodded 'yes', others 'no.'

"I saw where it was last night and they said that this is a billion year comet and that most likely its last visit to this part of the solar system was at Earth's formation!"

This statement received the attention of us all, "Good Lord!" we exclaimed together.

"It was here at Creation and now it has returned at Earth's destruction?" said Clara with a look of bewilderment on her face.

As we all stared at each other in shock, it dawned on me, "The heavenly signs!" I blurted out. "Remember just before the great battle of the Lord, that the heaven would be shaken and the stars fall? What happens if the Earth passes through the tail of a comet?"

"What?" asked Clara.

"A meteor shower," I replied.

"But they are harmless," declares Drow. "No more than a bunch of shooting stars; nothing to get upset over."

"Maybe, maybe not," said Lee. "It remains to be seen. The update last evening said we will definitely pass through this comet's tail but that we might chance a direct encounter with it on a closer scale, like maybe a direct hit. Or if not that, at least large meteors falling that are large enough to cause major damage."

"Which will be worldwide," finished Larraine.

"Plus," Lee added, "if you'll look towards the east you can now see the comet without a telescope or binoculars. It appears to grow larger every few days and is moving really fast."

I shivered as I felt a tingling sensation travel down my spine.

"Alice, are you cold?" asked Clara taking note of my shudder, for she sat next to me at the dining table.

"I think someone just stepped on my grave," I replied using the old allegory. My thoughts on the matter I decided to keep to myself, for to speak them would bring open conflict with some and I had no proof, just ... a feeling.

For a long moment all were silent as we each contemplated what was before us. We had already been through so much and were still suffering from the effects of the one nuclear-bomb that had made it to the United States. Millions had died in one second and the radiation surrounding that area was making millions more people sick. Our skies were still dark from volcanic ash and the dirt that was thrown into the atmosphere by both the volcano and bombs made matters even worse. I was amazed that we still had radio and some television. My thoughts on the matter were that we were intended to see what was going on in the world by ... someone.

Later, as I watched my small battery operated television, (I could only get the three main networks, like we did in the nineteen fifties) there was breaking news of major fighting in the Valley of Megiddo. It was so deadly that the Chancellor was forced to evacuate the Temple and was being flown back to Italy.

It was also reported that he took the Art of the Covenant with him, believing in its power to protect those that had it in their possession. So far it seemed to work for he escaped when others did not.

For the most part the Temple was abandoned, except for a dozen or so Goveian guards. No sooner had the Chancellor left the area than the Temple began receiving direct hits and we watched as it was quickly destroyed! I was amazed at that! I was sure the new Temple would survive but it didn't. Even the Wailing Wall came down and the area where all the Temples and the Place of Worship had once stood now looked like virgin ground and level. Nothing remained!

Smaller battles also were breaking out all over the world as people tried to get enough food to eat and fresh water to drink. As the weeks passed, the chaos got worse. There were reports of cannibalism in areas of the Middle East, most of Africa and parts of Asia. Most instances were in very remote areas that had not been reached by relief groups, a few of which did still exist such as the Red Cross, and others with which I was unfamiliar.

Even here at home, getting food was a daily chore. Growing it ourselves was impossible, with the ash cloud blocking out the sun, we knew we too would be starving in just a matter of time. Our only salvation was the food banks and grain bins, that we, like Joseph centuries before, had stockpiled several years' supplies.

These areas' locations were kept secret and were under military guard. Once again vouchers came into use as food was rationed. At the National Guard Armory where food was distributed, fights often broke out as people pushed and shoved to be first in line. All over the nation, this same scenario was repeated as guardsmen would be forced to intervene and some people had died, either shot by the guardsmen or beaten by the crowd who would not allow anyone to try and get more than their fair share of food. These long lines were under the scrutiny of the Guard.

My sons, Art and Lance became the providers in our family as they took on that role, for Thomas, Lexis and me. Lexis would often go with them to help carry our allotments back home.

Our horses and carts were still a very important part of our daily survival and their needs were as important as our own. They received parts of our grain allowance and our well water so far was uncontaminated. We considered ourselves blessed and we prayed hard each day that He would continue to watch over us and provide, until?

Chapter Seventeen

Our struggles became harder, day-to-day living was a trial in itself! Our meals were bland, consisting of grains, such as rice, wheat and my favorite, oatmeal. There was no sugar or milk and the grains were stewed in water and then eaten. Any kind of vegetable was very scarce but once in a while we could gather dandelion greens from the yard. I never dreamt I would eat lawn weeds, but dandelion was a tasty green leafy vegetable and the easiest to grow in low light. Mushrooms also played a large part in our diet and often had the texture of meat when used in cooking.

We still could get meat, but it was supplied by local hunters, who would shoot deer, squirrels or rabbits and sell the meat at road side stalls, the way farmers used to sell locally grown vegetables.

Rats and mice also showed up on the menu and were the cheapest meats that could be found. Cockroaches too were plentiful and many times these insects would be cleansed and fried alive in very hot fat, a high protein addition to a very limited diet. I tried some once, it wasn't bad but just the thought of eating insects of any kind was enough to sicken me to my stomach. It was a delicacy that we avoided! We hadn't gotten that hungry yet and I would rather eat the weeds out of the yard first!

The price of everything was very high and the US dollar was so devalued that it now took hundreds of dollars to buy what one dollar used to. It was so worthless that goods would be exchanged rather than use currency.

Unless you were in the military, more likely than not, you were out of work. There was no pretence now of wealth, even millionaires found themselves existing on what their own hands could produce. Their money was worthless. Now the term, 'all men were created equal' meant just that.

The nation came together as one and fought the hardships together. Man began to look out for each other in this land! They had no choice; the worst of mankind came to the forefront early and were 'weeded out' as it were by their own selfishness, which generally cost them their lives.

We pulled together, and we prayed. What else did we have? There's an old saying, 'there are no atheists in lifeboats!' When we were losing everything we had, we regained our faith!

The comet came closer and broke through the dusty layer of the atmosphere and could be seen as clearly as the noonday sun. But we could hardly pay attention even though we all knew it could mean the destruction of the Earth if something jarred it the least little bit from its path.

In the middle-east, the war now became nuclear, as the warring factions no longer cared about the survival of the Earth itself and in mindless thought, only desired to come out the victor! But to win a war at any cost means you have lost! What did you win? Scorched land that for thousands of years would be unable to support life?

The comet now stayed in the sky both day and night, its brilliant tail streaming millions of miles into space. It was hard to tell night from day now, even though we could see the sun, it always looked like it was just visible behind a brown cloudy sky, but at least we knew when it was daylight.

The fiery glow of the comet's head could be seen pulsating as it threw off bits of itself and as these pieces fell towards the Earth, the sky was filled with millions of shooting stars!

Now, some of these 'stars' actually made it through the atmosphere and began hitting the ground creating sporadic fires around and about. We were hard put to extinguish these fires but we managed to keep their destruction limited. Thankfully, not many made it through to the ground. They were both beautiful and terrifying to watch!

This phenomenon went on for weeks, it became so commonplace that we no longer took much note of it and still the comet grew larger in the sky. Then one night, we were awakened by a distant roar that grew louder in volume. It was a sound I had never heard before, kind of like rushing water, only echoing.

I woke Thomas and at that precise moment, our room lit up from a light coming in through the window although I had hung heavy drapes. We both hurried to the window and pushed opened the curtains and miniblinds and just as quickly closed them.

The sky was on fire! High over our heads and burning like the ceiling of a house, with the flames leaping skyward creating for us a burning roof! But none of the fire fell, it all shot out into space. I felt my heart race and wondered if this was it. Surely the oxygen in the atmosphere would be consumed and we would suffocate. As quickly as we could, we plugged up any holes that might draw our precious air from our house. We were alone! Cut off from all our relatives. For no one in their right mind would venture out into this!

So, we waited; and waited; and watched the heavens burn. It was only Thomas, Lexis and I. We lost television and radio. I had never felt so isolated and abandoned in my life. Outside, our horses dropped in their tracks and died. There was nothing we could do but watch. The house became uncomfortably warm and we feared that at any moment it would burst into flame and burn us alive!

So, we waited, and we watched, and we prayed, and just as suddenly as it started, it stopped. It only lasted for about forty eight hours! It was so dramatic that we were plunged into pitch blackness, a horrifying ordeal in itself! To be with constant light for twenty four hours a day then suddenly, nothing!

We peeped outside. The sky was clear, black and empty, except for the moon! The moon was huge as if it had come closer to the Earth and it was red, blood red! There were no stars! There was no comet! What had happened?

We had no way of finding out for we were still without any kind of communications, still no TV or radio.

"I wonder if it will be safe to open the door." I asked Thomas.

"No Grandma!" screamed Lexis. She was fifteen and most of the time was a very mature teenager that acted more like an adult than most, but now, she was a child. All during the last forty eight hours, she had clung either to me or her grandfather. We three had stayed very close together and had not slept in the bedrooms since awaking and finding the sky burning. In fact, we had barely slept at all.

At that precise moment there was a pounding on the back door.

"Mama, Dad, it's me, Lance!"

Lexis beat us to the door and quickly unlocked and removed the stuffing from around the frame of the door. Lance stumbled in. He wore his coveralls, gloves, and also had on a ski mask as well as a gas mask. He removed the masks.

"Thank God!" he exclaimed. "I see you did what I did! I wanted to come over but I knew I would die before I got ten feet from the house. I saw the animals drop dead! There's not a living thing anywhere. What grass or plants that were left alive, didn't make it through the inferno. I don't know how or why we did. Another day or so and we wouldn't have!"

I hugged my youngest son and cried at the same time. All during the last few years I hadn't broken down but now I did. I started crying and the others cried along with me as we stood and embraced each other. We knew that we had barely escaped with our lives! Did Art make it? Had any of my siblings? What about my neighbors? Furthermore what lay in store for us now? How many people had survived the inferno? If any were caught outside when it hit, unless they sought shelter immediately, they didn't stand the chance of a snowball in hell!

Then, we all heard the static of the radio and then a man's voice. We had tried the radio during the inferno and there of course had been nothing and we had left it on. Now we had proof of other life.

"... Ash was burned away by the flame." So we were about to learn what had happened. We hushed and listened.

"As the falling meteors from the comet were hitting the atmosphere, the ash and dirt suspended there caught fire and were burned away. The comet was completely dissolved when it hit the moon, knocking it into a lower orbit, and there was a very real danger of a collision with the Earth by the moon. It has taken on the color red, which is theorized to be caused by the particles suspended with the ice crystals in the atmosphere. The sky will from now on looks pink instead of blue and the moon blood red! The Earth now has many Saturn-like rings! We have escaped once again!"

Chapter Eighteen

Lance, why did you take such a chance as to leave your house so fast after the fire went out?" I asked after a bit.

The radio sputtered off as the batteries died. I went about the business of finding more, as I scolded Lance for risking his life.

"Mama, I had to know if y'all had made it through the fire. I looked out my window several times during the storm but the heat would make me close the drapes after a minute or so.

"I didn't ever see any movement over here and I didn't know if you had thought to plug up any holes. I thought about it after a few minutes, so I went to work cramming paper and rags anywhere I could feel a draft or suspected there was one."

"That may have saved your life," said Thomas. "What made you think of it?"

"Now don't laugh," he replied as he sat on the sofa with his hands dangling between his legs. His head was down, but now he looked at us from under his brows, which made me think of Daddy. "Someone told me to. I heard a voice from inside my head. It said to hurry. Then it said not to go out. A house doesn't have to fall on me, I did as it said. Why did y'all?"

"A fire burns oxygen, right," said Thomas. "We figured that with a fire burning the sky that it would take huge amounts from the air and since us human folks need it to breathe, we'd best try to keep what was inside, inside. It only made sense!"

"We can only pray that other people did the same," I joined in. "Of course some homes might be tight enough, this one is fairly well sealed; we only have to worry about the outside doors and the attic door. But I don't believe we would have lasted another day.

"I wonder how many animals survived." I thought out loud. "Two of my cats did, they just happened to be inside that night, you know I usually put the cats out at night."

"Mama, I saw the birds fall out of the sky, dead, almost immediately after the fire started. You know the horses are dead?"

I nodded, "Yes, I saw them drop. Did the fire cover the entire Earth? I guess we know that it was the comet hitting the moon that caused everything. I wish I knew more."

By now I had installed more batteries into the radio and tuned it to a clearer station.

"The planet has escaped being totally destroyed," said a woman's voice over the radio. "If you are just now finding our station, let me caution you and warn you to stay inside for another few days until we get the all clear from Homeland Security.

"Millions of animals are dead; their decaying bodies are polluting the atmosphere. The National Guard in hab-mat uniforms are now gathering the corpses of any animal, man or beast, and disposing of them in mass graves. They do not want to burn the bodies due to the low levels of oxygen in the atmosphere.

"Do not have any open fires, this by order of Homeland Security.

"The war in the Middle East has been forced to stop as soldiers by the millions dropped dead where they stood. Only those in enclosed areas survived.

"There was nothing that anyone could have done to stop the comet. Scientists thought it would pass millions of miles on the outer orbit of the moon and so on towards the sun. Instead it was drawn in by the Earth's gravity and had it not been for our moon, it would have hit the Earth and caused instant destruction.

The moon took the comet's direct hit. For some reason, the moon did not explode but instead cushioned the impact like a rubber ball and absorbed the energy by moving away. It was forced into a lower orbit. The orbit it had when it was first created billions of years ago.

The comet being mostly ice and dirt, was dissolved and the pieces spewed out into space but the Earth's gravity pulled the pieces back to it, and into orbit, creating Saturn like rings.

The mineral in the ice crystals and dirt is copper sulphate, which accounts for the red color of the moon and our pink sky.

The President has ordered all remaining men home from the Middle East. Although the land for the most part has been spared, the Earth's animal population, human and non-human is one-thirty-second of what it was. Almost all animal life is gone. Humans caught outside who did not seek immediate shelter, perished.

There had been sporadic reports of miraculous survival as people claim to have been warned by voices to take proper action to seal up their homes and to remain inside. A few said they saw angels.

As you might imagine, the polar ice caps melted; as they did so the water levels rose but this also released oxygen back into the atmosphere replenishing what had been lost. It was, *is*, our one saving grace. We might have lost some beach front property but right now we need oxygen more than we need land."

So, we lived, but our situation was even worse! We no longer had our horses for transportation. The only way to get anywhere was on foot or bicycle.

Art showed up a few days after the ban on outside travel was lifted, riding on Little Art's bike. I cried when I saw him.

"Mom, I had to know if y'all survived?" he said as we hugged him. My sons and their families had made it through the inferno. Art said that it was the children that told them that an angel had warned them what they needed to do. I felt chills when I heard that.

"Mama, Brook described a man wearing a white dress that was down to his knees. He had red wings, and carried a pot of some sort. She said that he glowed like he was on fire, but the strangest thing is, she saw him before the inferno started. She was in our bedroom when the light came in through the windows and told us what to do and when we wouldn't do it; she threw one hellayious fit until we did."

"Thank God, y'all listened to her or you might have died," I said between my sniffles.

"Well, after we saw the birds dropping and the other animals falling out of the trees, we knew that we had just witnessed a miracle!"

"Lance and I are going to ride to our other relatives and friends to see how many made it through. He's taking Alexis' bike. We might be gone a few days, so don't worry about us. I have my gun and we are taking food and water with us. I can't stand not knowing what is happening with everyone."

Although I was told not to worry, that was all I did. They were gone for a week, but late one afternoon, they came riding their bikes up my driveway.

We learned that most of our family members made it through, a few did not. Those that didn't were caught outside and were unable to seek shelter. We would mourn them. But all my siblings and their spouses made it. I had no idea when I would see them again for we were all in our fifties or sixties and weren't able to ride for long distances on bikes. (Heck who are we kidding? I can barely walk with my bad knees and we're talking about riding bicycles!!!)

The United States government, under pressure from its citizens was forced to release the remaining supply of gasoline, with the warning that this was the last of it and when it was gone there would be no more until the oil fields in Alaska were once more producing. This was the last of the stockpile that was kept for national emergencies. We had gas and it was enough if rationed properly, to last the nation for a couple of years.

So about a month later I did manage to visit all of my sisters. We all lived within an hour's drive before the energy crisis so I thought we should be able to manage it if the roads weren't in too bad a condition.

It was rough I'll admit, most of the time we rode on dirt with plenty of potholes in the pavement that did exist. We knew we wouldn't make this trip again for a long while. We left very early and took food, water and other necessities for survival, should we become stranded somewhere, you never knew.

I made it to Anne's first, then Larraine's, then Clara's, for she lived the furthest from us. We weren't able to go to Colin's and Drow's; we couldn't have done it all in one eighteen hour day. It was an all day trip.

We shared our experiences of the night the inferno started and all had heard the voice in their minds, telling them what they needed to do. Anne is the only one to see the angel and she even carried on a conversation with him. She described him as a glowing being in a short white frock, with white very short hair and red wings.

"He spoke to me in my mind," Anne said. "After he said what we needed to do I asked him was Jesus about to return? The angel said to watch the sky in the east that a light would show there. Then he disappeared!"

"Well, I think it is very close" I confided. "I don't know how much longer the Earth and its people can hold out."

I could only stay for about an hour with each because I wanted to visit them all in this one day.

They each told me how thankful they were that Art and Lance had come to check on them. I bid them 'goodbye' and headed home.

Chapter Nineteen

Our world no longer resembled the world we lived in just three short years ago. It was as though we had slid backward on the waves of time. The only remembrances of our former lives were the skeletal remains of our decaying structures. Yes, it looked like the aftermath of a nuclear war.

Scared? I was terrified! Although like millions of others I managed to conceal it, for what was the point? There was nothing I could do. This was too big for any one person or even a group of people. Our resources were so diminished that cavemen would have been in better shape than we were. They at least had the vegetation and wild animals to aid them in their day to day survival.

Where were we going to get sustenance and even housing for millions? I did not have the answer and our government was struggling after losing so much of the military. We were at the mercy of the world and the world gave no mercy!

Through the bits of information I gathered from the radio and the occasional television broadcast, we learned that the Goveian in Asbath had declared Asbath now the capitol of the Earth and the Chancellor as sole ruler. He was God, he said, on Earth, just as Jesus had been! Plus he had his war machine intact and the Ark of the Covenant to ensure his supremacy over the world.

He now was demanding a tax on the Earth, in the form of gold that any nation might have, that was once used to back their currency, which was now worthless. In exchange he would see that they were fed and clothed and their homes rebuilt. They must swear allegiance and worship him.

And many did; but the United States, Britain and Canada refused and were now deemed enemies of God and scheduled for eradication!

"There is a new astral event being seen in distant space," said the man in a wrinkled shirt and a day old beard. He looked as if he hadn't slept in days.

I was amazed that this one network could still get onto the air, and it was not one of the three main networks we were used to. No, this was one of the all news stations that had relocated from New York City to the mid-west where the countryside was open and did not present too many barriers for their signal to be telecast by their satellite trucks.

They had fuel that the government had given them to help get the news out to the population. They were bouncing their signal off of the moon. It was now in an orbit just a few hundred miles above the old orbits of the communications satellites that were destroyed in the Inferno.

"Our large observatories are showing a rip in the fabric of space. It is as thought the sky is opening up. Now there is speculation that it could be a wormhole, a term used many times in science fiction novels and movies, which describes a link between two universes. So far it is much too soon to elaborate on the significance of this event and our scientists are waiting to see if this continues to develop!"

Unable to talk with any of my siblings, I had only my own thoughts as to what was happening. Lance, who lived just across the way from us, was the only one I saw every day and he would sometimes stay overnight, sleeping on our sofa.

Our countryside was no longer green but brown and gray. No longer could I see squirrels frolicking about in the trees. The trees now stood leafless and charred. No birds filled the now clear but cloudless pink sky. It had stopped raining and all we had was the relentless sun that blared down on us.

The blood red moon went through its cycles as before, only now, our tides were over fifty feet high and came further inland by as much as a hundred miles in some low lying countries. We now lived within twenty three miles of the Atlantic Ocean whereas before we were about seventy five miles from the nearest beach. People no longer left their homes, for there was no place to go.

Many skyscrapers had had their tops burned off but people who live in single or two stories homes were the lucky ones, they still had a decent roof over their heads. We considered ourselves part of the lucky ones, for our home remained intact and our well still gave safe drinking water.

"There have been reports of people disappearing," said the same man, only this time he was cleaned up and in a suit.

This statement of course drew my immediate attention. What did he mean by 'disappearing'? Were people being kidnapped? And if so, why? My mind drifted to the darker side of human nature and remembering the cannibalism that had been reported in other countries made me consider this possibility here.

"This might have gone unnoticed except that prisoners that are religious fanatics, as labeled by the Church, are some of the ones that have vanished.

"Another prisoner began screaming when his cell mate faded away and just a specter of the man rose up and through the ceiling of the cell! Almost all of that prison's inmates that were religious prisoners vanished.

Also reports of people degenerating into translucent images of themselves have been told by ordinary people who then watched as they lifted up into the sky until they were no longer visible."

My mind drew a blank, what on Earth was going on? Was this some kind of new weapon that singled out certain individuals and did away with them but had no effect on the rest of the population? I began to think that this was a conspiracy by the Goveian to do away with religious and political prisoners and have something else blamed for it.

Now everyone kept an eye on the phenomenon happing billions of light years in space. The Earth's strongest telescopes were trained on it and it was growing larger rather quickly.

"They are saying that something has emerged from the rip, it looks like a huge white cloud with a bluish glow emitting from its center which is sending out electrical sparks. Some scientists are saying it is a nebula-a huge cloud of stellar dust which is usually left over from the explosion of a star. In this case it would be from millions of stars. Scientists are baffled at what this astronomical phenomenon can be.

"Some are speculating that a reversal of the 'Big Bang' might be about to happen although this event was not supposed to happen for billions and billions of years."

"Alice," it was Anne.

I had seen her car drive up the driveway and she was followed by Clara in her car with our brother, Carter.

"C'mon in," I called.

"We're in," she replied.

Clara, and Carter came in behind her calling, "We're here too!"

No sooner had they sat down than Lee and Larraine drove up.

"How did everybody figure to come today?" I asked as I saw our two brothers drive up together. Soon Colin and Drow were inside and laughing at how we all had the same thought.

Since food was scare, everyone had thought to bring something to help stretch my meager supply.

"Well, Sis," said Anne, "You should know that we all need to be together right now. I wish the phones would function again."

"Well so many of the phone lines were destroyed; it will be a long time before they will be repaired. Many, many people either died during the Inferno or else have simply disappeared, there's not too many left who know how to do the repairs. I'm just grateful we have radio and TV!"

My sisters and I managed to put together a meal of stewed squirrel with mushrooms and rice. I hadn't eaten squirrel since I was a very young child when Daddy would bring them home from a hunting trip. I remember watching Mama skin and clean the squirrel and how she stewed them with plenty of black pepper. Mama loved black pepper and often over-seasoned some food with it but I had grown to love it like that and still use plenty in my own cooking.

Colin had furnished the squirrels and he had already skinned them and dried them, "I went hunting on my property and bagged as many as I could and dried them to preserve them," he said. "It is the only way to keep meat now. I shot them before the comet so there's not much left in my smoke house. I have some rabbit and some deer meat and that's about it."

"You were smart to think ahead like that," said Lance

"Drow helped me," he replied. "I don't let anybody know that I have meat. You know what would happen if they did. It wouldn't be pretty."

"There isn't any wild game left now," said Thomas. "I was never much of a hunter myself, didn't see any reason for it, until now that is."

After we had discussed how we had survived the inferno, with many saying how good it was that it had happened at night because most of us had been inside. People on the other side of the globe weren't so lucky for it was daylight and many were caught outside and hadn't managed to get to shelter in time. Many more had died there than here!

Chapter Twenty

"Lee, what do you make of this new 'whatever it is' in space?" I asked. "You think it might be another comet?"

"Naw, it isn't a comet, it is much too large," Lee replied. "The scientists think it might be a wormhole but there's never been one seen before. They don't know if they really exist, it's only Einstein's theory which makes way for the possibility of wormholes. This is the first time that one has actually been seen and scientists do not know what to make of it. And that cloud came through it and I think something is hidden inside of the cloud."

"What?!" Clara asked, all of a sudden more than a little interested.

"Maybe it is aliens," answered Drow with a grin.

"Well, we would be foolish if we were to think that we are the only intelligent life form in the Universe," stated Lee. "I have always believed we are being visited by aliens."

"Could it be something else?" I asked.

"It's anybody's guess," said Lee.

"Well, it is billions and billions of light years away and if it weren't for the high powered telescope that they'd just built a few years before all this madness happened, we wouldn't even be aware of it now," said Drow. "I don't think it has anything to do with us and we have nothing to worry about, not something billions of miles from Earth. We have enough problems trying to survive!"

"And at that distance and considering the speed of light, we might be seeing something that happened thousands of years ago," I added.

To which we all agreed and changed the subject.

Yes, we had more important things to discuss that affected us much more than a nebula way out in space.

"You know, we now have plenty of sunlight, I think we should start growing some fresh vegetables," said Anne.

"And to be sure, some food animals survived. All of the livestock certainly didn't perish. After all farmers and even ranchers will have barns where some of the animals may have been and survived. We must look into all possibilities because we are looking at starvation in just a matter of months if we don't," this from Larraine.

My siblings left just before dark and it was kind of sad to see them leave, but at least I knew they were well and making plans to save our families, for we knew we couldn't rely on others or the government for much longer. We had two years to get back on our feet or it would be over for us as families and as a nation.

Slowly the weeks passed, and we all were so busy surviving that before we knew it, several months had passed. Our government had not relented to the Church's demand so we were pretty much on our own.

But the Chancellor was making for himself surroundings that rivaled any monument ever created for any ruler. He carried on as Chancellors always have with their religious duties and now he had taken to making laws, and not just for Asbath but the entire planet.

"A state of emergency has been declared," said the reporter. "An army is gathering in Asbath. The Chancellor at his news conference held earlier today, nine o'clock PM local time, has stated that the Earth is coming under attack by invaders from the far reaches of space."

This was a morning news program I watched as I sat and drank my morning cup of coffee. I was dumbfounded, what was he talking about? I hadn't heard a word of this before now. I continued to listen.

"It seems that the nebula has not remained stationary in that region of space and has advanced more than two thirds of the distance towards Earth. Scientists now agree that craft or ships are hidden inside of this cloud. The Goveian, as ruler of Earth, and having the only intact army is preparing to meet this threat head on. In fact nuclear missiles are now being calibrated to launch at the approaching enemy should it come within the boundaries of the Milky Way."

"Oh this is silly," I said aloud. "Even if we are about to be invaded from outer space, the Earth is incapable of defending itself from that kind of advanced technology. It's a lost cause!"

A knock at my back door later that afternoon proved to be a Nash County deputy sheriff.

"Good afternoon, Madam. I am taking a census of Nash County, may I come in?" he asked as he showed me his credentials.

I allowed him to enter and we sat at my kitchen table and drank strong black coffee that I had made that morning and reheated. Coffee was too scarce to throw away and I used grounds at least two times, and sometimes three, if it was only me wanting a cup.

"We need to know just who survived. How many are in this household?"

The questions were very personal and direct and the withholding of known information would be punished by a fine of a hundred dollars.

"How many children?"

"One, a teenage girl of fifteen."

"Are you married or widowed?"

"Married."

"Your husband's name and age and health condition?"

"Seventy four and no major health problems, just diabetes, high blood pressure and back problems."

"He doesn't qualify," he mumbled.

"Qualify for what?"

"Military duty."

"Military duty? What are y'all doing, building up the army?"

"Yes madam. Well, I have enough information and I thank you," and with that he left.

I tuned the radio until I found more local news, attempting to find out exactly what was happening here at home. Not only here at home but across the nation, the military had been so depleted when the Inferno struck, that it left this country defenseless. We had many of the military bases left intact but very few men left to man them.

Since so many had died at once, knowing who survived was difficult. The government now was taking men who had at one time been rejected. They were scraping the bottom of the barrel as it were.

Lance would go, Art would not. Many of my sister's sons and daughters and grand children over eighteen would now be drafted. Plus draft registry was required for any child from twelve to eighteen and their address must be reported each year. At the age of fifteen they would begin receiving military training and any with the potential to become officers would be singled out and given special training.

I sat with my head in my hands, bowed in a silent prayer. Had we reached our end? With our prime population going into the military, how were we expected to produce the food crops needed to prevent starvation? Was the government planning something and hadn't revealed it yet?

The next three to four weeks saw the departure of our young men and women heading for boot camp. My heart broke, having to see my youngest being driven away on a bus. But I was not alone in my despair, for many shared this fate.

I sat bolt upright in bed, started out of a deep sleep. At first I couldn't distinguish the sound I was hearing. Lexis came into our bedroom at just about the time Thomas woke and sat up.

In the darkness I could just make out her form as she spoke, "Grandma, what is it?"

What it was, was a siren.

"We're under attack!" exclaimed Thomas.

That had been my thought as well, but by whom? We rushed into the living room as the siren rose and fell in a rhythmic beat that was unrelenting. Covering our ears helped little.

"Missiles have been launched," declared the announcer. "News from the Goveian stated that it had become evident that our boundaries of the Milky Way had been breached and at a very rapid pace. It is obvious that the planet has come under a serious threat from the Nebula."

Second Event Chronicles

Then the announcer paused, he placed his hand over his ear as if listening, "I apologize, this is just in," and a sheet of paper was placed in his hand by someone out of camera range.

"The Nebula has not only reached the edges of the Milky Way but, at this reporting, is within the outer limits of our Solar System. Fighter jets have been ordered into the air. Any nations with any military armament are ordered to be on standby."

Chapter Twenty-One

Lexis began crying, "Grandma, I'm scared!"

I consoled her as best I could, "We need to say a prayer for I do not think we can stand against what is coming before us!"

Thomas not being much for praying aloud left it to me, "Our most gracious heavenly Father, You know our needs even before we do. I ask for your divine protection and intervention and help this nation to choose wisely, Amen."

At that moment, the lights came on in the house, the phone began ringing, the radio playing, and the big television in the living room lit up. We hadn't had electrical power for over a year and now every electrical device we owned began operating.

Plus the telephone was ringing; Thomas answered it and then hung up. "It was the phone company letting us knows that the phones are working."

"But where did the electricity come from?" I asked not really expecting an answer.

Our attention turned to the big TV as it began changing channels on its own. We had almost all of the networks on the air. Finally the picture came to a halt on my favorite news' channel.

Then the phone, "Alice," it was Anne. "Our electricity came back on and the phone is working. I wanted to let you know."

"I know, Anne. The same thing happened here. I think it has happened all over the country. Maybe things will get better now."

"I'm going to hang up and call everybody else."

"I think maybe they know already," I laughed. "If that siren didn't wake them, the lights coming on surely would have. But let me know what you find out, bye!"

"Goodbye!"

"We are receiving pictures from the telescope that has been focused on the Nebula."

As the announcer spoke we were shown pictures and what we saw was very familiar looking, for it resembled many of the nebulas already seen hundreds of times from the Hubble telescope, which now of course no longer existed.

"A few weeks ago, this un-named nebula was as harmless looking as any seen before but the unusual behavior of this one leads scientists to speculate that it is being guided by intelligent beings. There's a very real chance that unknown and possibly hostile beings are hiding in its depths."

The reporter went back in time over the past several years and discussed everything from the outbreak of World War to the natural disasters; the shortage of fuel, and the comet colliding with the moon, and the fire that burnt the sky, which rid the planet of the dust cloud that encircled it, blotting out the sun.

All the while the siren screamed. When it finally stopped at about three in the morning, it was as if time itself stood still. Everything was so quiet; I realized that my ears were ringing. We were so tired that we all went back to bed. Whatever was happening was not going to affect us for a few hours maybe and we could get some much needed sleep.

But daylight brought more interesting news; I flicked on the lights, made coffee, and turned on the Saturday morning news. This felt like old times and I could get used to it rather quickly!

"Disturbing events took drastic turns during the night while this country slept. The Goveian has split diplomatic relations with the Jehamic nations and they are now threatening to destroy one another.

"It seems that the Religious Groups' leaders had not wanted missiles launched as early as they were. Their reasons being that it was much too soon to do any damage. Plus, the Jehamic leaders had voiced concerns that Allah is inside of the Nebula.

"The Asbathian Principal Leaders deny the existence of Allah and accuse the religious Groups of blasphemy against the Chancellor, as God on Earth.

"War has been declared! The two allies are now fighting each other."

I was stunned at this turn of events, my mind wandered away from our own survival and to the survival of the planet itself. The planet was barely supporting life as it was, now with the prospect of more war which might once again spread around the world, the likelihood of any recovery and improvement in our circumstances was remote at best.

I turned off the news programs and searched for something that would take my mind off of our immediate problems. But the trouble was, no new programs had been made and the best I could find were children's cartoons.

The day waned, and my nerves began to fray, how much more could a body and soul take? Just when things began looking up, they began to diminish again.

Oh well, whoever said life was fair?

We watched every day as the cloud-like nebula crossed our solar system; one by one the planets disappeared into its mass, now we could plainly see it with the naked eye. Our young men and women were ordered to prepare for an aerial attack.

The Asbathian Principal Church turned its full attention on the nations of Jeham, determine to destroy them and take possession of the oil fields, knowing that then the whole world would be at their mercy.

Then, out of nowhere the cloud-like mass threw off its camouflage; it was now maybe a thousand miles or less from Earth. At first we thought a huge thunderstorm was in the making. The wind blew, with lightning flashes and rolls of thunder, but no rain.

Fighter jets took to the sky; missiles were launched from every nation that had them, except for a few, the coalition of the United States, Canada, Australia and Great Brittan.. For some reason these countries held back, refusing to take part in the Chancellor's War.

At first when the cloud dispersed, you saw nothing, just pink sky and no clouds, just as before. You could just make out the jets soaring across the heavens and the missiles exploding like so many fireworks that you might see on the Fourth of July, only more spectacular.

Then astonishment, as forms took shape, emerging from nothing, appearing out of thin air. It was awesome! It is the only way I know how to describe it.

I saw angels! I knew them to be angels although they did not have wings as you might expect, which for some reason did not surprise me! They held flaming swords. Their skin was bluish-white, their hair burned with blue fire, their gowns were pure white, and they soared like eagles. There must have been hundreds of thousands of them. They were much too numerous to count. The heavens were filled with angels, angry angels, for they struck the jets from the sky, tossing them aside like toys.

They swooped, and dived and came very close to the ground. Their faces glowed, and shimmers of heat rose from their bodies, as they fought with the armies of man.

The battle continued for much of the day. As fascinating as it was to watch it was most terrifying as well; we continued our observation from inside, at the windows.

I knew now what was happening. Although there had been times when my faith had wavered, for it seemed that the promise of Christ's return would never happen, now I knew it had not been in vain, for I was seeing with my own eyes that event taking place.

Now the armies of man had been defeated and I thought the battle was won but no, some beings more sinister took up the fight. They had hind legs like goats, and horrid disfigured faces and they spat green bile from their mouths, bile that disintegrated anything that it touched, as a strong acid might.

But the flaming swords of the angels cut the daemons in two and each living half fell to the Earth and writhed about in agony, because as immortal creatures, they could not die.

Humans took shelter wherever they could and the news cameras kept filming the battle taking place aloft. We sat at our televisions and watched as the battle waged.

The fight continued into the night and by dawn's first light you could see the living corpses covering the

Earth. Now surely the battle was won - but no, there was to be more!

Now the heavens were clear and only angels circled above, but as the sun peeped over the horizon another took up the challenge, a huge dragon, about the size of the largest dinosaur that ever lived. He had mottled red scales, two powerful hind legs and two smaller arm-like limbs in front. He had two bat-like leathery wings and fire billowed from his mouth and nostrils.

Again a figure appeared from the clear sky, a rider on a white horse, carrying a bow and upon his brow sat a crown. His face was radiant and shone like the sun, his eyes were white without pupils, and his white garment was smeared with blood. He charged the dragon and shot an arrow straight and true, it hit its mark, into the heart of the beast, and the dragon had not a chance.

As he fell from the heavens he changed, no longer a fearful dragon but a fallen angel. Lucifer, as he once was, in all his glory and beauty, once known as the bringer of light. He fell a great distance with his hands holding the arrow that had pierced his heart, yet he could not die.

Another angel appeared, one not seen before, his garment was the color of clear water and he carried a huge key, he and a host of angels grabbed the fallen angel and supported him, as a chain of purest gold was wrapped about him and the key used to lock the golden chain.

Now the sky split, which is the only way I knew how to describe it, for a section tore and peeled away revealing a hole of blackness! Here the fallen angel, Lucifer, and his demons were taken and tossed into what looked like a bottomless pit in the sky. His struggles were useless and his unearthly screams sent chills through your very soul. Now his conspirators, the fallen angels that had followed Lucifer in his attempt to take the throne of God, were thrown into the pit with him. Then the sky closed and once again was blue.

However, the Earth was still covered with the dead of Man, and birds once again filled the sky and flew down and around devouring the flesh of the fallen.

Once again our attention was drawn to the heavens, for the King on the white horse was drifting down toward the Earth and with him were the twenty-four elders, and following him was a multitude, they were clothed in white, they had crowns on their heads, and then the King had set foot upon the Earth, on the Mount of Olives in Israel.

The multitudes were singing, and it was a song of praise and of worship. Christ had returned! Alleluia!

The End!

And the beginning of the...

'Millennial Chronicles'

The cameras stayed focused on Jesus and his entourage of angels. All set down on the Mont of Olives, then in a grand procession, they marched towards the destroyed city of Jerusalem and the location where the temple once stood, which was now so much dust and rubble.

In my way of thinking, Christ could just wave his hand like a magician and everything would miraculously repair itself in the blink of an eye, but I was wrong it would seem.

No, our God and His Son, Jesus were very patient Deities. Was not the Universe billions of years old? And Man did not appear on the scene for millions of years more. No, when you are the beginning and the end of time, the alpha and the omega, then you do not hasten your creation. Time, as they say, is on your side.

To be continued...

Printed in the United States
83836LV00003B/154-156/A